THE PACT

THE PACT

CHRIS IWEGBU

The Pact

Copyright © 2019 by Chris Iwegbu. All rights reserved.

No part of this publication may be reproduced, stored in a retrieval system or transmitted in any way by any means, electronic, mechanical, photocopy, recording or otherwise without the prior permission of the author except as provided by USA copyright law.

This novel is a work of fiction. Names, descriptions, entities, and incidents included in the story are products of the author's imagination. Any resemblance to actual persons, events, and entities is entirely coincidental.

The opinions expressed by the author are not necessarily those of URLink Print and Media.

1603 Capitol Ave., Suite 310 Cheyenne, Wyoming USA 82001
1-888-980-6523 | admin@urlinkpublishing.com

URLink Print and Media is committed to excellence in the publishing industry.

Book design copyright © 2019 by URLink Print and Media. All rights reserved.

ISBN 978-1-64367-486-5 (Paperback)
ISBN 978-1-64367-485-8 (Digital)

Fiction
06.08.19

Chapter 1

Obinna Kelechi left the 4th floor of the office building known as the Bureau House in the city of Lagos, Nigeria, having just attended an interview for an advertised job—a job he desperately needed. The building, which housed a number of small and medium sized mostly-ailing businesses, itself, was in dire need of renovation. He walked wearily down the roughly-tiled stairs, not caring to use the elevator, as he knew the elevator does not work. His facial expression was pallid and exhibited a gloomy aspect. He suffers from occasional, irregular twitches of his facial muscles. This was something he was used to, but on this occasion, the twitches were accentuated and more frequent perhaps caused by the unsatisfactory manner the interview was conducted, and more importantly, by the hunger pangs which gnawed pitilessly at his stomach. He understood why he suffered hunger pangs—it was almost forty-eight hours since he had his last meal—a very frugal meal of dry corn bread and one unripe orange. He was used to hunger pangs; but what he was not used to was the dull ache in his head. He had woken up feeling slightly faint with the headache early in the morning but had done nothing about it. Really there was nothing he could do as he was unable to afford even the most basic healthcare, or a visit to the hospital. Languidly, he moved down the stairs, as though in a dream, more or less dragging one foot in front of the other. His knees knocked occasionally though he was slightly bowlegged. His entire bearing gave anyone who saw him an instant impression of a very despondent man with little hope left in the world.

THE PACT

Obinna stood approximately six feet and one inch from the ground. His severely lanky frame was suggestive of a desperate want of adequate nourishment and care. He looked much older than his forty-two years. His head was of massive proportions, somewhat incongruent with his lanky body. Within the enormous head lies a very sharp brain; a brain he had put to good use in his education by graduating with flying colours from the University. He had graduated at the top of his class almost two decades ago in the field of Philosophy. However, in spite of his excellent qualifications, he was unable to find a job. His luxuriant hair, which was once very dark, had all virtually turned silvery-grey. It was recently cut short with money he had borrowed from a friend, after much entreaty, to enable him look more respectable for the interview and possibly more employable. His eyes were large and coffee-brown in colour; restless eyes that never missed anything in the vicinity, and absolutely resolved to finding a job opportunity for their languorous owner.

Lacking money to buy newspapers, he would stand for lengthy hours at news and magazine stands free-reading articles with keenly alert eyes and mind for job advertisements. His one and only care in world was to get a job and enjoy some of the good things of life—at least the ones money can confer the ability to enjoy. As for relationships with the opposite sex; he found it difficult to start or sustain any. Naturally shy and awkward with women, he would rather be elsewhere than with a woman. Nevertheless, he had been in few relationships all of which ended sadly because he could not meet even the least demands of the ladies. His last girlfriend, Monica, was a thirty-year old fun-loving woman who had simply walked out of the relationship without attempting to tell him why. Obinna did not bother to ask because he knew the reasons why she walked away. He knew it was mainly because he could not afford to give her anything meaningful or worthwhile. She had complained about this to him, bitterly, on several occasions as she found it difficult to comprehend or appreciate his difficult circumstances. Unable to take it any further, she merely stopped communicating with him and disappeared from his life. He had not bothered to ask or look for her. That was about a year ago, but the last thing in his mind now was to get another girlfriend. "Job before woman" he had told himself repeatedly.

He reflected angrily over the interview he had just attended. Although, he had given satisfactory answers to the questions he was asked, he knew he stood very little chance of getting the job the moment the Chairman of the Interview Panel asked him who was backing him for the job. Obinna had replied very calmly, "Nobody." The way the Chairman shook his head with disdain instinctively told Obinna he stood no chance of getting the job. He had been through these kinds of interviews several times in the past that he knew what the outcome would be just by studying the expression on the faces of his interviewers. Obinna's eyes had run across the desk, rapidly scrutinising the faces of all the members of the interview panel seated at the desk. He could faintly perceive the subtle scorn and mockery in their eyes. This caused his heart to sink. The sinking of his heart drowned the last vestige of hope he had had of getting the job.

"Thank you for coming. We shall contact you if need be," the Chairman had said very grimly to him.

Obinna felt a painful pang in his chest as his heart missed a few beats. His first thought, after the Chairman's remarks, was to reach out for him, squeeze his scrawny neck, and choke him to death. These kinds of thoughts do suggest themselves to Obinna from time to time when he feels insulted, even slightly, by anyone else because of his circumstances or when he perceives an infringement upon his rights. However, he had never yielded to these brutish thoughts.

With a great effort, Obinna had drawn himself up from where he was seated, mumbled his thanks, and shuffled out of the room. As he backed the Panel of Interviewers, and walked towards the door; he seemed to feel the presence of a thousand hostile eyes peering through the back of his massive head.

At the end of the stairs; he stepped into the street, instantly took a deep breath, and filled his lungs with fresh air. How refreshing it felt to him to be out in the open air than breathing the damp air of the Bureau House. However, he felt ill as the dull heaviness in his head throbbed painfully. He had endured this sick feeling and headache all day. Ignoring these symptoms; he quickened his strides slightly as he walked down the crowded street, eagerly observing the various commercial activities being carried on in the streets with keen interest.

He stood momentarily, watching the different vehicles on the road, and listening to their blasting horns. At the opposite side of the road, not far from where he stood, he spotted a magazine stand. Instinctively, he started walking towards the magazine stand with a vague expectation of finding a job advert in any of the magazines. As he stood, waiting to cross the road, he became suddenly lightheaded. His heart raced wildly, fluttered, and cold perspiration broke out suddenly upon his forehead. His facial muscles started twitching very rapidly. His vision suddenly dimmed and quickly progressed to total blackout. Obinna screamed for help as he fell, facedown and senseless, to the ground.

Chapter 2

Obinna opened his eyes and looked very slowly around him. He became slightly agitated as it dawned on him that he was lying down in a hospital bed. He could strongly perceive that typical antiseptic odour that characterized hospitals. The dull ache in his left arm drew his attention to the arm, and was surprised to find an intravenous infusion or drip connected to it via tubes and fastened by plasters. The label on the infusion reads, *5% Dextrose Solution*. Not sure he knew what that meant; he looked away from his arm, and his eyes strayed to one side of the room. He saw a chair beside the bed. Seated on that chair was an immaculately dressed man who appeared to be dozing. He could hear the faint rhythmic snores from the throat of the stranger. He looked carefully at the stranger but could not recognise him. Then gradually the memory of what happened came flooding back to him. He remembered the interview, how he stood waiting to cross the road, how he felt suddenly ill, then what?

"What next?" He asked himself half-aloud. That sick feeling was the last thing he remembered. "How did I get to this hospital and onto this bed?" This question and many others were begging desperately for answers in his mind. He shot another look at the stranger on the chair, and cleared his throat deliberately with a loud sound with the intention of waking up the stranger. "Perhaps this stranger might have some answers to the questions plaguing my mind," he muttered to himself.

The sound woke up the stranger; he raised his eyes and looked in Obinna's direction. He saw Obinna sitting up in bed then smiled at him instantly, a sympathetic smile, which exposed a set of excellently white teeth.

"Good grief!" The stranger exclaimed, "You are awake." He stood up gently from the chair, then, in a very friendly manner, said: "My name is Joshua Anjorin Babatunde but my friends simply call me Josh."

"Pardon me, Mr. Joshua Anjorin Babatunde, but who are you?" Obinna asked earnestly as he scrutinized Babatunde with his eyes, "And perhaps you know something about how I got into this hospital?"

"Yes," replied Babatunde somewhat heartily, "I brought you to this hospital." Then with a voice that rang out his words in very clear accents, Babatunde said, "I was drinking beer with some friends of mine in a bar near the Bureau House when I noticed a sudden panic amongst the crowd in the street." Here, Babatunde paused for a few moments to study Obinna's apparently bewildered face.

However, the friendly smile on Babatunde's face seemed to reassure Obinna, warming his heart, and putting him gently at ease that Obinna relaxed the confused look on his face. This encouraged Babatunde to continue his narration.

"Amidst the crowd," he said, "You were lying facedown and unconscious. In the ensuing confusion, the people around you tried vainly to resuscitate you, they yelled for help and tried to figure out what else they could possibly do to bring you back to consciousness. I saw what was happening from the bar, and instantly perceived the helplessness of the people trying to help you. Without wasting time, I got into my *Toyota Camry* car drove through the crowd, lifted you into the car, and drove you as quickly as I could, straight to this hospital."

Obinna studied this obviously kind man in a very curious manner, and noticed that Babatunde's looks were impressive. He was strikingly handsome and tall. He had a pencil-line moustache, was very fair in complexion, had a small narrow mouth bounded by two thin lips with a nose that looked more European than

African. His eyes were brown and tinged with blue. He was gorgeously dressed in native attire and wore a very sweet smelling perfume. On the surface, Babatunde looked like a very wealthy man—well fed and highly successful—with an air of authority around him which was boldly accentuated by his every bodily movement. He looked like someone who was very happy and contented with life. Obinna thought he and Joshua Babatunde were probably about the same age. However, in terms of looks or appearance, they were polar opposites: while Babatunde appeared handsome and well-nourished; Obinna's appearance was plain and haggard for many years lack of adequate nourishment and care. And perhaps because of his good looks, Babatunde appeared much younger.

When Obinna finished his silent assessment of Babatunde's appearance, he started slipping into his usual melancholic state as bitter jealousy began taking root in the innermost recesses of his heart.

"Why is life so unfair?" He asked himself silently and angrily. "Should I call it fate? Curse that fate! Why should this stranger—Joshua Babatunde—be so apparently blessed with all the good things of life while some people are left with very little or nothing at all? Can anybody ever judge life or fate as fair?"

Questions of this nature were running rapidly through Obinna's mind, and were gradually being reflected openly in the deepening grimace on his face. However, he quickly reminded himself that this stranger, whom he barely knew, and was beginning to dislike, had actually saved his life. Then with a great effort; he controlled himself by essentially uprooting the sprouting jealousy in his heart, flinging it away, and thus, forcing himself to assume a more amiable facade. Undoubtedly, Joshua Anjorin Babatunde was a man who readily inspired jealousy in others, especially in less fortunate and less endowed individuals who would not stay contented with their own lot in life. People turn their heads easily in the streets to get a second or even a third look at him any time he was seen in public. However, these were extremely rare occasions as Babatunde rarely left his house. He had a natural charm that was almost uncanny, and which drew certain personalities to him while others were instantly repelled. He was mostly begrudged for his wealth and good looks by many.

"I guess I owe my life to you. Thank you very much." Obinna said to Babatunde in a calm manner having successfully suppressed the rising anger and jealousy in him.

"Oh, please, do not mention that," replied Babatunde, "It was such a pleasure…nothing makes me feel better than lending a helping hand to anyone who would accept my help."

"However," Obinna said in an earnest voice after a slight pause, "I know that all you've done for me must have caused you a lot of money. But the truth is I have no money to repay you now. Please, you just have to give me some time to raise the money."

Babatunde ignored his remarks.

"I have introduced myself to you," Babatunde said to him, "I think it's time you return the favour, please."

Obinna stared blankly at Babatunde then looked slowly away.

"My name is Kelechi…Obinna Kelechi," he said somewhat timidly, "There isn't much I can tell you about myself save that I've just been existing in Lagos city without employment, living daily from hand to mouth, for many years now."

He paused here momentarily and looked shiftily at Babatunde, hoping to see the impact of what he had just said on his face, but was rather disappointed as Babatunde's face remained expressionless. He continued the introduction with a ring of self-pity in his voice.

"I am a university graduate," he said, "I made first-class in the university but have not been able to find any job since. Attempts to start my own business went on the rocks on four occasions. Life has been pretty rough with me, Babatunde. Many times I have had to beg to eat just one meal a day. But I want you to know, my friend, that in spite of all the hardships I've been through in this life, not once did I ever consider crime as an option."

He finished the last sentence with an expectant look in his eyes as though he craved, or expected to be applauded for his refusal to engage in crime in spite of all the reasons he had to have embraced it heartily. But there was no response from Babatunde.

At this point, there was a slight knock on the door, and it opened gently to allow in a doctor followed by two nurses. The doctor was a bespectacled middle-aged woman in scrubs with a stethoscope dangling across her neck. She was in her forties, but was free of wrinkles, and still looked beautiful. The two young nurses with her, also in scrubs, were obviously in their twenties, and were very pretty. Their faces glittered with radiant smiles as they entered the room.

The doctor greeted Babatunde courteously, turned her head towards Obinna, and greeted him.

"I am glad to know that you have regained consciousness, sir." She said to him.

"Thanks," Obinna responded rather unenthusiastically.

"I am Doctor Maria Onwuka-Smith," she told him, "And I am the Medical Director of this hospital—St. Mary's Hospital. It is nice to have you here, sir."

"Thank you, doctor."

At this point, Doctor Onwuka-Smith turned towards Babatunde, asked him very nicely to excuse her for a few minutes, then suggested that he could wait at the hospital's reception till she was done with Obinna.

Babatunde thanked the doctor, stood up instantly and left the room.

The doctor then proceeded to take Obinna's medical history, something she could not do when Obinna was rushed into the hospital in an unconscious state a few hours ago. Babatunde, being just a Good Samaritan, could not volunteer much useful information on Obinna. Thereafter, she proceeded to examine Obinna.

"Well sir," the doctor addressed Obinna after completing the examination, "I cannot detect any sign on physically examining you. However, when that gentleman—your friend—rushed you in here, we took your blood for analysis. All the test results are here with me." She produced a sheet of white paper, showed it to Obinna, and said in a sympathetic manner: "All the test results turned out negative except for one—your blood glucose level—it was very low. It was below the critical levels for the sustenance of life; that was why you became suddenly unconscious, and if your friend had not made it here quickly enough, the outcome would have been very grave indeed."

When she finished speaking; Obinna looked up at the doctor, and all he could do was to admire her secretly. He thought she was a very nice and good looking woman. The way she was explaining everything so nicely to him suggested that. His eyes also went on to assess the two pretty nurses beside her. He thought that the world with more of people like Doctor Maria Onwuka-Smith and her lovely nurses would be a much better place. However, he knew this was not the case as his various experiences in the world had convinced him that the world was full of people who were selfish, arrogant, envious and malicious. He forced himself out of this brief reverie and expressed his appreciation to the doctor with as much sincerity as he could muster.

"By the way," continued the doctor, "It is unusual for the blood glucose to fall so dangerously low, Mr. Obinna. Your test results and medical history revealed very little to me. I am obliged to subject you to further medical evaluation to find out what really happened—perhaps there is an endocrine pathology or a malfunction somewhere that must have predisposed you suddenly to such a potentially-catastrophic event. It is necessary to find out the cause and manage it effectively in order to prevent a repetition."

Obinna lay motionless on the bed, and did not respond for a while. He seemed to be very busy with his thoughts. The only visible sign of movement in him was his facial muscles which suddenly twitched, stopped and twitched again. Obinna knew that he was as healthy as a top-class prizefighter; that he rarely fell ill; he knew that he had been literally starving. Why, he ate his last meal over fifty hours ago, and what a poor meal it was—just a small piece of bread and one little orange. Moreover, he had gone without food for almost forty hours before that meal! But how could he admit to this charming doctor that he was so wretched and could not even afford to feed himself? He told himself that a man must always maintain his pride and not appear weak and helpless before a woman.

"Emm... doctor, ...emm," he stuttered when his silence was becoming awkwardly prolonged, "You see, doctor..." he forced himself to cough lightly, "We are observing seven days of dry-fasting in our church. I happen to be one of the Elders of the church, and, therefore, I must always show good example to the congregation."

"Oh I see," replied Dr. Onwuka-Smith understandably, "It is clear you've been starving yourself, Mr. Obinna." However, she quickly cautioned him in an earnest voice, "While respecting every Faith and never belittling the doctrines of any Church, I believe we should not adhere slavishly to every Church doctrine or practice especially those that may be potentially injurious to our health or cost us our lives. For this reason, we were endowed with the faculty of reason by God, and given a freewill to know when to draw the line. I personally believe in the 'Middle Path' in all the circumstances of life, for me, it is the best path, and that is what I choose all the time when I need to make a decision. I am also recommending the, 'Middle Path,' to you, Mr. Obinna. Try it, I promise, you'll not regret it."

Obinna, unwilling to flog this issue or discuss it any further lest he be caught in an embarrassing lie, readily agreed with the doctor's suggestion.

"I absolutely agree with you, doctor," he said, "Next time, I just have to draw the line."

"Alright, Mr. Obinna," the doctor smiled and said, "All your vitals are stable now. We'll observe you for just twenty-four hours then discharge you afterwards if you still remain stable."

"Please, doctor," he protested gently. "I feel stronger now than I have ever felt all of my life. I'm itching to get back home, and finish a very important assignment I was working on. I am fine as my test results revealed, and I've explained the reason for the low blood sugar to you. I would really like you to discharge me home now, doctor."

Dr. Onwuka-Smith silently considered his plea for immediate discharge.

"Well, alright, Mr. Obinna," she said after a while, "We shall observe you for only twelve hours after which I shall discharge you if you remain stable. And please, Mr. Obinna, no more protests."

"Thank you, doctor." Obinna responded reluctantly without sincerity.

He would have been more grateful if Dr. Onwuka-Smith had granted his wish for immediate discharge as he was sorely troubled about the bills. He knew that the longer he stayed in the hospital; the larger would be his bill. He had every reason to be concerned because he was more or less always penniless. He was afraid of being embarrassed at the time of discharge as he had no money on him. He secretly hoped that his new friend, Joshua Anjorin Babatunde, had sufficient cash on him to settle the hospital bills. He told himself that he would refund Babatunde later. Thereafter he wondered if the doctor's decision to discharge him in twelve hours, against her initial intention of twenty-four hours, was a demonstration of the middle-path philosophy of life she so believed in and had just recommended to him.

"Mr. Obinna," Dr. Onwuka-Smith interrupted his thoughts, "We'll leave now to let you rest. But my nurses will be coming back to check on you at regular intervals till we're satisfied."

"Thanks, doctor," he mumbled.

Thereafter, the doctor signalled to the two nurses and they all turned and left the room.

Chapter 3

Obinna and Babatunde left St. Mary's Hospital in Babatunde's car immediately after Obinna was discharged from the hospital by Dr. Maria Onwuka-Smith. Obinna was completely occupied with his own thoughts. He had never met anyone quite like Babatunde all his life. Not only did he owe his life to him, but Babatunde had paid all his hospital bills willingly without asking to be refunded. Immediately after he was discharged, and as they walked towards Babatunde's car, Obinna had pleaded with Babatunde, in a very earnest voice, asking Babatunde to give him some time to enable him raise the money for Babatunde's refund.

However, Babatunde had waved Obinna's plea aside, and merely told him to forget about the money. In all his life, Obinna had never met anyone so kind that he felt completely overwhelmed by Babatunde's kindness, a kindness that left him breathless and speechless for some time.

"Is this guy for real?" Obinna had asked himself several times. "If he is for real, then he must be one in a million...nay, one in a hundred million for the world is filled with very selfish and wicked people, this fact, I know first-hand."

Babatunde drove the car out of the hospital onto the road, increasing its speed gradually as the car raced on for about twenty minutes till it started slowing down steadily, turned and entered the parking lot of *Tasty Treats Restaurant.*

"Please, let's eat here," Babatunde said, "I am hungry and I suppose you should be too." This was the first time he was speaking since they left the hospital.

"Hungry is an understatement," Obinna responded with a happy ring in his voice as Babatunde parked the car and switched off its ignition, "I am completely famished."

Soon, Obinna and Babatunde were seated opposite each other at a table in the restaurant and were eating a delicious meal of assorted fried foods: rice, chicken, fish, and beef with salad. The meal was accompanied by various types of cold fruit juices, Coca-Cola and many other exotic drinks. Babatunde had ordered a double portion of food for Obinna, and also told the waiter to prepare a double portion of packaged or takeaway food for him. Babatunde ate very slowly, and barely consumed a quarter of the contents of his plate, though he drank more of the juice. He watched Obinna most of the time, and seemed slightly amused at the way Obinna was eagerly shovelling the food into his mouth, scoop after scoop, till his plate was completely empty. He pushed that plate aside, and started on the second one with undiminished fervour. He ate till all the contents of the second plate also disappeared through his throat, and down into his stomach. Had he been offered a third plate, there is no doubt that Obinna would have also dispensed with it easily with a lot of pleasure. Thereafter, Obinna took a very long drink of icy-cold Coca-Cola, his favourite drink, and belched loudly afterwards. The sound he made when he belched suddenly caused a number heads in the restaurant to turn wonderingly towards them. Some of the heads had derisive looks on their faces as they stared at Obinna and Babatunde in amazement at the table. However, no one said anything.

"Excuse me," Obinna said quietly after belching.

Babatunde did not reply. He was busy having a very hard time trying to suppress a laughter that had welled up so enormously within him and was threatening to be let loose right there in the restaurant. Luckily, Babatunde succeeded in stifling the laughter; a laughter that would have been so ridiculous in the superfluity of its mirth, and would have caused more curious heads to turn towards them, had it been unleashed in the restaurant.

"Wow, thanks a million," Obinna said to his friend with a broad grin, "That meal brought me fully back to life. All the while, I wasn't really myself, I was only half alive. Oh, what an excellent meal! My mind and all my thinking faculties are open and clear now. I can talk and reason rationally now. Thanks once again, Babatunde. You are such a great guy."

Babatunde said nothing but merely smiled at Obinna. He was in high spirits, and seemed to be having such a great time studying and enjoying the company of his enigmatic new friend. Obinna took another long drink of Coca-Cola, but this time, he managed to expel the gas without making a sound.

When Obinna returned the glass to the table, he peered at Babatunde, and scrutinised him with his eyes.

"You look more like a saint," he told Babatunde, "More like a saint than a regular guy. I mean your looks—they are almost saintly. Then your generosity, just like that of a holy man, is completely baffling to me. I know there are no such things as saints; but such generosity as displayed by you today certainly qualifies you as one."

Babatunde did not say anything. He merely continued to smile wonderingly at Obinna.

"These days," continued Obinna, "No one gives anyone a helping hand. Not even siblings, no… not anymore; it was in bygone days…days of yore… that family members really cared, loved and helped one another. These days they do nothing but strut and fight all the time with materialism being always the root cause of their incessant quarrels."

"Materialism is in the heart of man," Babatunde responded, still smiling, "It is the very epicentre of man's existence. Imagine a world without materialism! What a boring world that would be. Perhaps the saints and holy men you mentioned a while ago, through a lifetime of effort, might mitigate its compelling power, but I don't believe it can be completely divested of the nature of man."

"I agree completely with you, Babatunde. Materialism has brought much progress to humanity. Mankind will be hundreds of years behind without it; in fact, we'll still be in the dark ages without materialism. Good thing there are no saints in the world to drum it out of us."

"You don't seem to believe in saints, do you, Obinna?"

"What!" exclaimed Obinna looking straight into Babatunde's eyes, "Don't tell me you believe in such a false concept as the existence of saints? That is absolute crap, a total BS!" After a slight pause, he said: "Oh, you are so credulous, Babatunde. Let me tell you a truth; the single truth about saints, holy men, churches, synagogues, temples, mosques and all the likes. Religion, in all its ramifications, was fabricated by smart men to deceive the gullible and the less intelligent ones."

"Really?" Babatunde queried, profoundly surprised at the assertions of his new friend.

"Absolutely," came the reply from Obinna, "And quote me anywhere else, Babatunde. Do not forget that I studied Philosophy in the University. I am also very well-read on these matters, and have an in-depth knowledge of the various religions of virtually every society and culture in the world. Religion was, and is still, my absorbing interest. I have proofs that can discredit all religions of the world, and label them for what they truly are, 'A scam of the wise to deceive the unwise.'"

"Obinna," Babatunde addressed his friend affectionately by name with a smile, he leaned forwards at the table, and said: "I find you very, very interesting; but these issues you just spoke so passionately and apparently very knowledgeable about are very sensitive ones. They are not what we can discuss here tonight. We have been in this restaurant for approximately one and half hours, and it is getting quite late. Let me drop you off at your apartment, and you can come and see me in my house any time at your own convenience. We can discuss anything there for as long as we wish. Here is my card," he extended his business card to Obinna, "Call me before you come so that you can be sure I am at home, though, I rarely leave my house."

"Oh, that apartment of mine!" Obinna whined as he collected the card from Babatunde, and pocketed it. His voice sounded miserable, disturbed, as though some kind of trouble awaited him at his place of residence.

"Is there any problem with your accommodation?" Babatunde asked him after eyeing him earnestly.

He met Babatunde's eyes but quickly looked away.

"You hardly know me," he responded still looking away, "But you have been so good to me as though you've known me all your life. I am already indebted to you a great deal. It would be unfair of me to transfer all my burdens to you."

An understanding smile instantly lit up Babatunde's handsome face.

"Look, Obinna," began Babatunde in a very accepting voice, "We are friends now and brothers veritably. I personally believe that nothing happens by chance…our meeting is not a chance occurrence by any measure but preordained by inconceivably giant forces. You must allow me to help you at every point of your need as much as I can because such selflessly rendered help is to our own mutual advantage. So, please, tell me about the challenges you have with your apartment."

"I live in a single room apartment in Yaba," began Obinna after a slight hesitation, still looking shyly away, "I'm six months behind in my rent. I have been desperately trying to avoid my landlord for over a week now because of his constant hassles. The landlord has threatened to evict me from the apartment if I don't pay up by the end of this month."

"How much do you owe the landlord?" Babatunde asked in a sympathetic voice.

"Fifty thousand naira," he replied bashfully.

"Very well," said Babatunde, "That is not too big a problem to handle." He suddenly glanced at his *Rado* wristwatch and said, "Please, let us leave now, Obinna. It is almost midnight."

Obinna quickly reached out and grabbed one of the unopened fruit juices on the table, opened it, lifted it to his mouth, and drained its contents to the dregs. Thereafter, he picked up two unopened Coca-Cola bottles as well as his double portion of takeaway food pack, and stood up from his seat whilst Babatunde went to the counter and settled all the bills. Afterwards, both men exited the restaurant walking side by side. They were a sharp contrast as they left the restaurant with all eyes glaring at them: the one… gorgeously dressed, handsome, confident and obviously wealthy; the other… shabbily dressed, beggarly, gaunt and timorous but curiously arrogant in demeanour. As soon as they entered the car; Babatunde reached for the glove compartment of his car, brought out a wallet he usually kept there, counted out a total of two hundred and fifty thousand naira, and handed the cash to Obinna.

"Take this money," Babatunde said to Obinna as he handed the cash to him, "Pay up your rent and use the rest for your upkeep."

Astonished beyond description, Obinna became dumbfounded once again. The events of the day, from the time he regained consciousness at St. Mary's Hospital, to the present moment, all seemed so surreal to him that he pinched himself severally hoping he would wake up from what he thought was an incredible dream. Babatunde saw him pinched himself but merely grinned. He knew what that meant. He knew Obinna was only trying to convince himself he was not in sweet dreamland. Obinna had never handled money this big all his life. Little wonder he was behaving so awkwardly. He hesitated in accepting the money, but Babatunde pushed the roll of money into his hand, started the car and drove away.

"Thank you," Obinna muttered in an almost strangulated voice as the car raced away from the restaurant.

Chapter 4

Obinna woke up around half past ten o'clock the following morning feeling a lot refreshed; though his bed, if it could be called a bed, was an old thin and worn-out mattress placed on the bare and hard concrete floor. The room was small, substandard and bereft of any furniture save for one isolated, half-broken, plastic chair in a corner of the room. At different places in the room were three small plastic containers, carefully positioned, to collect water that dripped from the leaky roof whenever it rained. The walls of the room were very damp and supported the growth of moderate amounts of mould. Obinna owned practically no property. His only possessions were his books and a few clothes most of which were already threadbare. The books were stacked, one on top of the other, and formed a huge heap on the concrete floor in one corner of the room. The books dealt extensively with subjects such as Philosophy, Biography, Government, Politics, Science, Economics, Astronomy, Religion and Mythology. Obinna was particularly fond of Plato, and had invested his time extensively in the study of Plato. The biographies of Winston Churchill and Thomas Edison fascinated him tremendously, and Obinna drew daily inspiration from reading them. However, many of these books which constituted his most cherished possessions were already being affected gradually by the profound dampness of the room. He was aware of this fact, but knew practically nothing about how he could protect his precious books. At another corner of the room were about two or three small black cooking pots, plastic plates, cups and spoons kept carelessly on the floor. These were his cooking utensils which served him well on the few occasions he decided to cook. These occasions were, however, very rare as he found cooking uninteresting, tiresome and time-consuming. Rather, he preferred to eat, when he had the money, from cheap roadside restaurants referred to in common parlance as *Mama put*. Not far from where the pots lay were the food pack and two Coca-Cola bottles he had brought home with him from Tasty treats Restaurant. He planned to steam the food later and eat it as breakfast. That was the reason for bringing the food home with him. His clothes were suspended on a hanger nailed roughly to the wall. Underneath those clothes were two, old, worn pair of shoes—the only ones he owned. The ventilation of the room was poor as there was only one window which made the air hot and stuffy. Over that window hung a dusty old and tattered curtain which served the purpose of shading the room a little from the harsh and scorching, silvery rays of the tropical sun.

The bathrooms and kitchens of the apartment building were situated outside, in a separate building, like an attachment to the main building, and shared with neighbours. The neighbours, on many occasions, had to wait their turns to use the bathroom. This crude arrangement had been the cause of many conflicts amongst them as some of the neighbours had the habit of complaining bitterly that the other tenants spent too much time in the bathroom, thus wasting their own precious time, especially on days they wished to get to their various places of employment, or offices in a hurry.

Obinna's apartment building was in a decrepit state, congested and squalid. Yet its owner seemed to enjoy nothing better than harassing and threatening his tenants when he was owed even as little as a month's rent. Not once had the thought of carrying out repairs in the building, or improving its aesthetic value, entered the owner's avaricious mind. Any tenant who complained about his or her room was told to leave outright by the landlord.

"Pack out of my house!" The landlord would yell at the complainant in a most contemptuous manner, "You add no value to the house... we'll be glad to be rid of a scum like you!"

Thus was the bad attitude and inappropriate behaviour of the landlord. He knew that because of the outrageous demand for accommodation in Lagos, if anyone of his tenants left any of his grossly substandard apartments, a potential new tenant usually showed up within forty-eight hours at the most.

Obinna, still lying on the mattress, reflected over all the happenings of the previous day. He still seemed surprised at all the events. He had fallen asleep the instant his back touched the old mattress on the floor of his room, after Babatunde had dropped him off the previous night around one o'clock in the morning. He sat up abruptly in his makeshift bed, dipped his hand beneath the pillow, and pulled out the roll of cash Babatunde had given to him the previous night. He smiled and counted the money carefully again for the third time. It still amounted to a total of two hundred and fifty thousand naira. For him, it was worth a king's ransom. He smiled again; with this money he could pay his irritating landlord the fifty thousand naira for the six months' rent he owed him. If he liked, he could pay the landlord an advance of another six months, or better still, leave the house for a more decent accommodation in a swankier part of the crowded city of Lagos. He would still have more than enough to feed himself very well and take care of his needs should he decide to leave his present unsatisfactory accommodation. The money, he reasoned, could last him for a couple of months if spent wisely. He felt relieved to know that he would not have to worry about his meals for a while. He rummaged through his clothes for the business card Babatunde had given to him, found it in his trouser pocket, pulled it out and examined it. Babatunde's name was written boldly on the card, and below his name were three cell phone numbers. There was no indication of Babatunde's business, office, or work place address on the card. That seemed odd to him as he had seen numerous business cards in the past, and what usually featured prominently in virtually all of them were the business names, professions and addresses of their owners.

"Well, that was quite an omission on the card," he said to himself after ruminating about it for some time, "But it is certainly nothing to worry about."

He then made up his mind to visit Babatunde in five days' time, and told himself he would bring the error to his notice. He was sure it was an oversight. He told himself that perhaps in the near future, when he had become more acquainted with Babatunde, he would ask his help for a job. He felt very certain that someone like Babatunde should be very influential, and would know a lot of people including very powerful politicians. He told himself that he would not mind working for Babatunde. After all, his theoretical knowledge of business was very sound. He would apply as Business Manager to Babatunde's fleet of businesses, and he felt very sure that Babatunde would grant him the offer once he made the proposal to him. Obinna felt very happy, something that was not common with him at the time because of his incessant troubles. In fact, he was almost ecstatic at this point. He was certain that the end of all his hardships and sufferings were in sight. Indeed he had caught a glimpse in his mind's eye of the end of the vast sea of woes, embarrassments, and sorrows he had been swimming in.

"At last!" He shouted very excitedly to himself. He jumped out of his mattress, laughed aloud hysterically, clapped his hands, and shouted again, "At last, a light has been lit for me at the end of the hideously dark and seemingly unending tunnel that I have been grovelling in for many long years now!"

Moments after Obinna had shouted so rapturously to himself, and while he was still deeply entranced in this euphoric elation, a very loud and deeply disconcerting knock was suddenly heard on the door. Obinna snapped instantly back to reality. He looked at the door wondering who could have knocked his door so loudly and so disrespectfully. Curiously, he started walking towards the door; in order to open it. But before he could reach the door, it swung open suddenly on its own, and a fierce looking man entered the room.

The man was fat, short and squat with a large protruding abdomen. His face was round with two large bulging eyes, thick lips and a very fleshy nose. Above both eyes were very thick eyebrows and protruding lashes that had all turned grey. His head was large, completely bald, and his facial appearance was that of a man in his seventies, or older. He wore a cream-coloured, wrinkled, short-sleeved shirt which exposed two huge fat arms covered with a thick growth of black and grey hairs interspersed. He wore a pair of dirty shorts which also revealed two fat hairy legs; and at his feet was a pair of bathroom slippers. The man looked menacingly at Obinna.

"Are you tired of hiding?" He asked Obinna in a loud croaking voice, "You dirty, never-do-well wretch; are you quite tired? Why, I've been looking everywhere for you in the past one week, and all you do is to hide and cleverly evade me! You watch what I'm going to do to you in a few days' time—I'm going to throw you out of my house—if you don't pay up the rent you owe me by next week! Pack out of my house, you dirty loafer! Not only will I kick you out, I'll make sure that…."

"Heh… heh… Mr. Fatai Johnson, stop! stop!!" Obinna shouted, interrupting the stranger, "Save your breath; save your breath, please, Mr. Johnson! I have your rent here with me now; here it is!"

Mr. Fatai Johnson, as the stranger had just been addressed, watched amazedly as Obinna drew out the roll of money Babatunde had given him the previous night. Obinna counted out exactly fifty thousand naira, and handed the money over to him. Mr. Johnson instantly snatched the money away from Obinna's hand as though he feared Obinna could suddenly change his mind about the payment. He counted the money carefully, then repeated the count more carefully and slowly the second time. After satisfying himself that the money was complete on the third count, Mr. Johnson's face suddenly lit up with a smile revealing a set of repulsive, brown, tobacco-stained teeth.

"Why, Mr. Obinna," he said, "Sorry about my initial outbursts. But you know how these things are… you know I have three wives and eighteen children. I need money to feed them. That's why I don't take very kindly to any of my tenants who owe me money. You know I have no other job… sorry eh… I will send your receipt across tomorrow."

Obinna did not say a single word. He merely listened and watched while Mr. Johnson addressed him. There was a deep, scornful expression on his face. He could perceive the strong, mixed odour of tobacco and alcohol in Mr. Johnson's breath. He was certain that his long outstanding rent, which he had just defrayed, would soon be gone with the winds—to be sadly and recklessly squandered by this landlord—on more cigarettes and booze and possibly, women.

Obinna was right; for he knew that was the kind of life his landlord, Mr. Fatai Johnson, lived. Mr. Johnson was a civil servant who retired almost ten years ago. He had managed to build his thirteen-room, two-storey, apartment building—his only investment—before he retired. He and his three wives with their eighteen children occupied only four of the rooms—each woman with her children in one room—while the fourth room was occupied by Mr. Johnson himself. The remaining nine rooms were rented out to tenants, and Mr. Johnson lived exclusively on the rent and his meagre pension which was never regularly paid. Since his retirement almost a decade ago; all he does is keeping the company of the neighbourhood's riffraff, drinking large amounts of beer, consuming vast quantities of goat-meat and fresh-fish pepper-soup, smoking packets of cigarettes everyday and actively engaging in womanizing. True, he had a large family; but Mr. Johnson hardly cared about his family. His family was a dysfunctional one; as dysfunctional as any human family could possibly get. He engaged regularly in squabbles and fights with his older children; while his very young children, who were still toddlers, barely recognized him. They don't call him daddy because he does not spend sufficient time with them. To those children, he was just another face, among the numerous other faces, they see around the old apartment building. Mr. Fatai Johnson stays out very late every night, returning very drunk, then to sleep till late in the morning. Once he's awake; he goes about bullying his tenants, harassing those who owed him money to pay up or get thrown out. The three women he married were much younger than him with an average of about twenty-five years; and they all had to work very hard, engaging in various petty trades and activities, just to cater for themselves and their little children. Although, he hardly gave anything to these women, Mr. Johnson always managed to extract a meal or two from them everyday—usually by prolonged coaxing, cajoling, flattery, and if these failed—by coercion. It appeared the only reason why these women stayed married to him was the shelter he offered them. On the days the women quarrelled with one another, usually over trifling matters, they disrupted and caused such an uproar in the entire neighbourhood that anyone just visiting the neighbourhood, and who was not familiar with them, would think a third world war had suddenly erupted.

Obinna stood, his coffee-brown eyes still fixated on the door, as Mr. Johnson, after apologising for his uncouth behaviour, and carefully pocketing his rent, had retraced his steps out of Obinna's room, quietly shutting the door behind him.

"What a miserable mistake of nature this man, Mr. Fatai Johnson, happened to be," Obinna said with a sneer on his face.

His eyes, which were still focused on the door, suddenly blinked and relaxed.

"Can anyone be more possibly annoying than Mr. Fatai Johnson?" He asked himself very thoughtfully, "Just a few minutes ago, I felt very good and happy with myself, now this errant landlord of mine comes in here and spoils it all for me."

Mr. Fatai Johnson had completely ruined Obinna's mood. His facial muscles started twitching abruptly, stopped, then twitched again before stopping finally. He decided he would quickly have his breakfast right away, refresh himself, then go out to unwind with a few cold beers. After all, he now had enough money in his pockets with some extras to burn. He picked up his takeaway food pack and a black pot, left the room, and proceeded to the kitchen to commence with the steaming of his breakfast.

Chapter 5

Five days later, Obinna stood waiting at the front entrance of Joshua Babatunde's large house. It was a huge, palatial building; magnificently built with glittering marble. A few meters from the main building stood the colossal statue of a lion, on a high pedestal, sculptured in pure gold, an excellent work of Art by all standards. Surrounding the massive statue, measuring about fifty meters in diameter, were numerous fountains of water; all spewing their fine, silvery-sprays upwards, far into the air, and then falling downwards, freely, in progressively widening circles into their source pool below. Connected adroitly at intervals to the statue and its fountains were numerous multi-coloured lights blinking intermittently at regular intervals, creating a spectacular appearance. The tremendous beauty of the golden statue with its surrounding fountains and attractively blinking lights never failed to charm anyone visiting Babatunde's house for the first time. Visitors would stand for prolonged periods, starring and admiring the scene, a scene some of Babatunde's rare visitors had coveted secretly in their hearts, and had desired for themselves. And when they had taken their fill of the scenery, they either advanced towards the massive building to gain admittance into the house, or retreated to the gigantic gate to take their leave.

Having previously called Babatunde on his cell phone, and informed him about his intended visit, Obinna was instantly admitted into the house by the Security. He was stunned by the dazzling beauty of Babatunde's house. He stood and watched the golden statue of the lion completely enthralled. After what seemed like an eternity; Obinna, with a tremendous effort of the Will, shook himself free of its mesmeric influence, and slowly recovered his senses. Then he looked away from the statue and gaped at the building. He saw its huge and tall columns; the large, tinted, highly-reflective, bulletproof windows; the scintillating marble walls; the excellent blinds; the superb doors leading to very fine balconies with their exquisitely beautiful flowers; and the excellent terraces with their brilliantly manicured lawns.

Obinna felt completely overwhelmed by this superfluous display of wealth around him.

"Wow!"…He exclaimed presently… "Where is this place?"

The house contained fifty large rooms and ten living rooms. Each living room measured roughly the same size as a quarter of the size of an Olympic-sized, football field; while each of the fifty rooms measured about twice the size of a conventional, or standard room. The house was exclusively furnished within and without with exotic furnishings imported from twenty-five countries spread across Europe, North America,

Asia and the Middle East. The grand design and architecture of the building were foreign, Gothic. And its builders were contracted from three countries: Italy, Germany and Iran.

A male servant met Obinna outside, greeted him courteously, and ushered him inside the building. His first sensation, as he stepped foot within the building, was the delicious ambient temperature. It was neither too hot nor too cold, but synchronized perfectly with the human body temperature. He was led into one of the living rooms on the ground floor of the house, was signalled to sit down, and told quietly to make himself feel comfortable.

"The master will be with you shortly," said the servant who walked away leaving Obinna alone in the vast and tastefully-furnished living room.

He felt like an oddity in the midst of the superb wealth that surrounded him. Though he was decently dressed, having just bought a few new clothes for himself, he still felt ill at ease in the large house. Was the owner of this fabulous house, which looked like a veritable heaven on earth, the same Joshua Babatunde he had met just a few days ago, and who was very good to him? Would Babatunde still be as nice and as friendly as he was to him the last time they met, or would he scorn and ridicule him for his poverty and lack of success? Obinna asked himself many questions of this nature, and seemed a little nervous or troubled by them. Although, anyone meeting Babatunde for the first time would perceive instantly that he was very wealthy—he looked it without a doubt, it was written very boldly in his very physical appearance and bearing—but no one could have guessed the vast extent of his wealth correctly. Everything in the house, visible and invisible, seemed to proclaim silently, the enormous wealth of its owner. Even the gigantic sofa upon which Obinna sat was extraordinarily tender, soft, and seemed to embrace and fit snugly around the sitter. His facial muscles began to twitch as was common with him whenever he was agitated, alarmed, or sensed a threat or danger. The twitching persisted for a while, and then ceased abruptly. He turned his massive head upwards, and his eyes greeted the highly decorative and attractively branched Chandeliers which hung nicely and securely in the ceiling. The Chandeliers were fully lit, though the room was brilliantly illuminated by the fine rays of the sun. The tinted, high windows added a peculiarly-beautiful hue to the silvery rays of the sun that streamed through them. The entire ceiling gleamed with silver, and reflected everything underneath. However, on looking more closely, Obinna fancied he could make out the indistinct outlines of two or three trick-mirrors that merged perfectly with the glittering silvery roof. In addition, his naturally restless and acutely curious eyes discovered two secret cameras mounted at two carefully concealed positions in the small angle between the wall and ceiling, one camera in the eastern angle and the other in the western angle.

"I'm being watched," Obinna said quietly to himself, "What in the world could Babatunde possibly be doing with these secret cameras and mirrors fit only for the use of the Secret Service in his house?"

However, after a little while, he relaxed, and his suspicions about Babatunde began to wane.

"Every modern house these days are fitted with these kinds of gadgets," he told himself, "Perhaps they were installed to enable Babatunde monitor his numerous servants and house keepers who might be tempted to pilfer any of the exotic, enormously-expensive, shiny furnishings in his house."

With these thoughts in mind; his doubts about Babatunde had almost disappeared. Shortly afterwards, he permanently laid to rest all the suspicions and anxieties about Babatunde which his exceptionally keen senses had alerted in him.

A few minutes later, Joshua Babatunde with two elegantly dressed lovely ladies following in his rear, entered the living room where Obinna had been waiting. Babatunde, looking as handsome as ever, was immaculately dressed. On his face was an excellent smile; exactly the same friendly smile he had displayed when he and Obinna had been together and parted ways a few nights ago. This further reassured Obinna; and seemed to answer the question of whether or not Babatunde would treat him with disdain when they meet again. He stood up as Babatunde approached him, returned the smile as best as he could, and both men greeted by shaking hands vigorously.

"Welcome to my house, and good to see you again, Obinna," Babatunde said in clear friendly accents.

"Same here," replied Obinna, somewhat timidly, in a slightly tremulous voice.

"You are looking very good," Babatunde told him as he eyed him intensely, "Much better refreshed now than you were five days ago at St. Mary's Hospital."

That was not flattery. Obinna indeed looked somewhat better having put on a little weight; and some of the prominent hollows on his face, caused by lack of adequate nourishment, were barely visible now.

"Thank you very much," replied Obinna, "That was possible because of your incredible kindness and generosity to me... thank you, very much indeed. I owe my life to you."

Babatunde's smile broadened.

"Meet two of my close acquaintances," he said after a slight pause.

Babatunde turned towards the two ladies, and signalled them to come closer. They obeyed instantly.

"Juliette, Martha!" He said, "Please, meet my good friend here, Obinna."

The two cute ladies, one after the other, with charming smiles on their faces, shook hands with Obinna in turn (Juliette first, followed by Martha).

"Welcome, Mr. Obinna, and glad to meet you." Each of them said almost simultaneously.

He nervously took their hands in turn, said nothing, but merely smiled. He longed to say something to the beautiful ladies, a compliment, or whatever as they offered their hands to him—at least to return the courtesy—but he suddenly suffered from a transient and embarrassing inability to vocalize his words. His tongue seemed to cleave to the roof of his mouth, and words just simply failed him at the time. To hide his embarrassment, he merely bowed slightly to the ladies, and smiled nervously.

"We were just about to have lunch when you arrived, Obinna." Babatunde announced immediately after the rather awkward introduction. "Please, join us. Let us proceed to the dining room and have lunch together."

The four of them with Babatunde leading the way, the two ladies walking beside him, and Obinna following at the back, advanced slowly to the dining room.

The dining room was large and furnished with a huge glistening oaken dining table that could sit about two hundred persons. Various paintings and numerous works of Art adorn the wall of the dining room whilst the smooth shinning floor was covered with a rare Persian rug at the centre. The four of them sat huddled together in the vast dining room facing one another. Babatunde sat directly opposite Juliette, while Obinna sat next to him and faced Martha directly. About five servants, all dressed in white and black with a black bow tie, were in attendance in the dining room. A diversity of very tasty meals was served in abundance with numerous wines poured out by the attending servants. Thereafter the dessert was served, and consisted of various kinds of delicious, mixed native and rare exotic, fruits all of which formed an excellent banquet, enjoyed to repletion by the four of them.

While they ate, Obinna constantly stole furtive glances at Martha. He would look at her, and then look quickly away if he had the slightest inkling that Martha was going to return his look. At one time, an unintentional eye contact sustained for a few seconds between them, left Obinna horrified and feeling like someone who had gazed directly into the eyes of

Gorgon Medusa. His nervousness with women was very profound indeed. However, he seemed curiously affected by Martha's appearance.

Martha was an exceptionally beautiful woman. Her dark, long and shiny hair was beautifully braided and packed neatly at the back of her head in a long and tidy ponytail. Her forehead was high, giving her a confident and noble look without any hauteur. Her eyes were very clear and bright like those of a child. She was tall, nicely curvaceous and attractively slim. Her voice always had a touch of pathos, reflecting her very sensitive and highly sympathetic nature. She was graceful, always good mannered, with a childlike innocence. Martha, though twenty-eight years old, was doing very well as an Accountant in a thriving Bank in the heart of the Lagos Metropolis, but was unmarried and still lived with her parents. Perhaps her greatest assets were not her physical attributes or accomplishments, but her deep spiritual convictions. Martha was devoted to her Catholic, Christian Faith and tried as far as was possible to observe the doctrines of the Catholic Church. The main reason, evidently, why she was still unmarried was because of her obstinate refusal to succumb to the pressure of having premarital sex, a thing demanded by every man who had attempted to woo, or show any serious interest in her.

"I need to try you out in bed before I commit myself," virtually all the arrogant and pitifully lustful men she had met in her life had said that to her; and often vocalized in a most lascivious manner. Many had even told her blandly, "I must impregnate you… I need to impregnate you… just to ascertain your fertility before I can commit myself to marrying you in Church."

"What a ridiculous idea being suggested by someone who wants to marry in Church," Martha would say to herself, "The same Church that condemns fornication and all forms of sexual impropriety. What can possibly be more absurd?" Martha, virtuous as ever, in her response to these erotic demands would say very nicely and always with a faint smile on her beautiful face, "You know that it is a grave sin to engage in what you are asking us to do… indulging in such an act would earn us both 'Express tickets into hell.'"

The men, after many vain attempts, would give up in frustration and stop calling her on the telephone. While still growing up as a youngster in her teenage years; Martha's mother, a virtuous woman herself by all standards, had drummed it repeatedly into Martha's ears—literally planting it in the rich garden of her young feminine heart, by telling her over and over again—that:

"Any man who really loves you, and is worthy of you, will not pressure you into sex. Your dad was a very decent man, and never pressured me to have sex with him until we were married. Our love was consummated on our wedding night, and it was such an exquisitely beautiful and never-to-be-forgotten experience. And because we kept ourselves pure, your dad and I have remained ever in love, and the

Almighty had never ceased to bless us because of that."

That was the lesson that Martha's mom had so effectively succeeded in teaching her daughter; and Martha, in her own turn, had so absolutely imbibed the teaching that premarital sex, for her, was not even an option in any circumstance even if it meant remaining single all her life.

Juliette, on the surface, was the equal of Martha in terms of physical beauty, and attractiveness. Perhaps that was the reason they were drawn to each other in the University. They liked each other the moment they met. They were both students of Accounting in the University, and had shared the same room in their final year. They had remained, more or less, friends since the time they met at the University. However, Martha and Juliette were opposites in manner, behaviour and temperament. Juliette cared very little about Christianity—her self-professed religion—or any other religion or faith. She was a woman of the world with an eye open for all the good things of life. She had dated a number of men in the past—more for material reasons and the fun of it—than for any kind of serious commitment. She had virtually thrown herself at Babatunde the moment she met him. Babatunde's looks impressed her, but what interested her far more was his seemingly inexhaustible cash. Babatunde had spent a fortune on her already: her nice cars, houses, countless jewelleries, clothes and steady supply of good money, were just a few of what Babatunde had done for her. She had managed to get engaged to Babatunde, and ever since, had become a regular visitor to his house, at times, passing the night whenever she wished. She loved to visit Babatunde in the company of her friends, just to show him off, and astonish them with his enormous wealth. Juliette had persuaded Martha to accompany her to Babatunde's house on two occasions in the past. This was the third time she was bringing Martha to the house. Although, Martha had congratulated them so effusively during their engagement; however, for some strange reasons, Martha did not envy Juliette, or wish she was in her place. Something in Martha had distrusted Babatunde instantly the first time Juliette introduced them. Nonetheless, Martha had never openly displayed, discussed, or expressed her strange feelings about Babatunde to anyone.

After she finished her meal, Martha thanked Babatunde for the tastefully prepared and liberally served meal in her usual sincere and soft-spoken manner. Thereafter, in the same vein, she requested to be excused in order to attend a Church meeting.

"Sweetheart," said Juliette, "Do you really have to go to Church tonight? I thought we're both having such a great time here together. Please, stay here with me—just this one time—the Church will not miss you, and I'm sure, God will understand."

Martha, a little surprised, was silent for a while, wondering.

"Dearest Juliette," she responded very calmly, "Remember we agreed earlier today when you came to my house, and asked me to accompany you here, that I can leave when it is time for my Meeting. Please, Juliette, this is a very important Meeting that I cannot afford to miss. And moreover, I have already booked appointments with some people I will not like to disappoint."

This was followed by a discomforting silence.

"Alright… alright," began Juliette with raised voice and arms suggesting profound irritation, "Alright, Martha, you win. Have your way! I only wonder where this excessive religiosity will get you… what the hell! At your age, you don't even have a boyfriend, Martha. You can't possibly be more religious than the Virgin Mary herself… you need to wake up, girl, and take life more easy!"

Martha, feeling slightly hurt, did not answer. She merely got up slowly from her chair, picked up her bag, and left the dining room after a slight bow of her head. Few minutes later, the three of them still seated in the dining room, heard the engine of her car start and drive away.

"She pisses me off so easily these days with her excessive Christianity!" Juliette said with evident annoyance as she looked directly into Babatunde's eyes, "Martha is rapidly becoming a fanatic!"

"You were a little hard on her, my dear," Babatunde responded, "You must appreciate that we live in a world where we have a Freewill to do whatever we please, even the Freewill to do stupid things and pursue worthless ends."

With that ever-present whimsical smile on his face, Babatunde turned his head sideways, looked at Obinna who had witnessed what happened silently in mixed emotions.

"Obinna," Babatunde addressed him by name, "Please, I apologize for what happened here just now. But in your candid opinion, what do you make of the little scene that took place a few minutes ago between the ladies?"

Obinna hesitated for a few moments. He appeared to be thinking of how to respond to Babatunde's question. Then he sat up abruptly in his chair, and cleared his throat.

"I honestly believe that the young lady, Martha, meant no disrespect," he said with some concern. "I just feel she is misguided… to be so devoted to religion in today's fast-moving world, a dog-eat-dog world, where even family members go for one another's jugular; devotion to religion is such a sad waste of precious time."

Juliette, whose ears were strained maximally, listening to what Obinna had to say, suddenly gave vent to a shrill laughter.

"Perhaps, Mr. Obinna," began Juliette when her laughter ceased, "Perhaps you should try to convince Martha about what you just said. If you dare try, she will never speak with you again, and she will avoid you like the plague. Oh, I'm so worried about her. I fear she might miss life altogether because of her slavish adherent to Christianity… and she is fast becoming such a bore. Imagine, I have introduced not less than six very rich and nice looking guys to Martha… but she just can't seem to get along with any of them all because of Christianity! I'm really so… so worried about her."

Thereafter the three of them left the dining room, and went to relax in one of the living rooms of the house. Babatunde and Juliette got better acquainted with Obinna by asking him a number of questions about his personal life. If Obinna had initial doubts about Babatunde, as he had when he just arrived at the house, and was seated alone waiting in one of the large living rooms; such doubts were now absolutely laid to rest by Babatunde's excellent conduct and friendliness to him, for Babatunde seemed almost angelic in his demeanour. The three of them spent the rest of the evening discussing such general issues as Politics, Sports, Social issues and the world Economy over series of fine, tasty wines. When it became slightly dark, Obinna indicated his interest to leave. Babatunde insisted that he partook of supper with them before he took his leave. This was very agreeable to Obinna who always welcomed an opportunity to eat a free meal. Thus, the trio returned once again to the dining room to have supper. After the sumptuous meal, Babatunde instructed one of his servants to drop Obinna off at his apartment in one of his numerous superb cars. When the car reached Obinna's apartment, and as Obinna alighted from the car; the servant pushed a bulky envelop into his hand.

"My master said I should give this envelope to you," the servant told him.

Obinna was astounded, received the envelope from the servant, and thanked him excitedly.

"I will call Babatunde on my cell phone as soon as I get to my room." He said to the servant as the servant drove away.

When Obinna reached his room, the first thing he did was to open the envelope, and out came several bundles of money from the envelope. He was stunned, settled himself down, and counted the money. Not believing his eyes, he repeated the count; and then again for the third time, and on all the three occasions, the money amounted to a whopping one million naira! Obinna, out of excitement, nearly passed out.

Chapter 6

The rain fell pitilessly, pouring down in very large torrents from the heavily clouded sky. Ferocious winds felled huge buildings, shattered windows, uprooted mighty trees and flung them with a vicious force into apparent nothingness. It was a very pitch-dark night; the unrelenting lightning repeatedly lit up the night—tracing luminous, terrifying, zigzag patterns across the darkened sky—and intermittently illuminating the frightening carnage beneath the heavens. Wild, roaring thunder crashed repeatedly through the night, wreaking untold havoc: splitting gigantic mountains open; setting trees and buildings on fire; felling huge boulders from shattered mountains and skyscrapers; killing innumerable people and virtually everything that had life on the land and sea; uprooting sturdy, mighty trees and hurling them away like mere wisps of cotton wool. Volcanoes, hitherto dormant, became suddenly active and spewed tremendous amounts of hot molten lava, dusts, ashes and sulphur violently into the dark sky. Millions of people were scorched to death by the lava, and several more millions were choked to horrifying deaths by the thick ashes and dusts that hung in the atmosphere, and prevented people from breathing. The ashes and dusts further intensified the darkness more profoundly. Fierce, unremitting winds whooshed ominously like a million ghost ships on a mission of death: opening up graves; disinterring corpses and casting them recklessly upon the living; lifting up giant trucks on the streets and hurling them with unfathomable power far into the sky. The flood waters rose steadily as the unrelenting rain poured ceaselessly down, swallowing up everything in its path: buildings, bridges, trees, vehicles and drowning countless persons; causing absolute chaos on the earth.

"Nature is angry!" Screamed a woman just before she was swept away by the deluge. Nature's laws, that ought to guide man on how to manage and live successfully on the Planet, had all been violated repeatedly, rubbished, and discarded with impunity by man. Man, through his activities and ignorance, was relentless in bringing harm and ruin to his fellow man and to the Planet ultimately. He is completely blinded by egotism, and has shut God completely out of his activities. And as a punitive measure, Nature, like an angry Schoolteacher, is wielding the big stick at her stubborn and recalcitrant students. She had unleashed, through the medium of her powerful elements, absolute mayhem on unsuspecting humanity. And the extent of damage caused by Nature in her rage was incalculable!

People who were still alive shrieked and wailed profusely. Everywhere, there was the cry of death, the smell of death, the sight of death that brought utter desolation on the human race. With upturned faces and outstretched arms; the few persons still alive looked upwards to heaven, expecting some kind of divine help or intervention. Rather, more intensely deafening thunderclap after thunderclap came; more destructive gales; and more vicious rains answered the plea of the idolatrous, boastful, and unbelieving generation that merited nothing but destruction.

Obinna and his friend, Babatunde, were amongst the very few lucky ones still untouched by all the destruction being wrought by the elements. They were completely drenched in the rain, but had managed to climb a high mountain, to seek refuge on it; and it seemed they had both escaped the sheer destruction still raging on below. Holding hands atop the mountain, both men looked fearfully downwards at the catastrophe below which Nature had wrought on puny humans in her great fury. The sight was completely heartrending as their eyes beheld the massive piles of dead bodies at the foot of the mountain. Obinna, because he was completely exhausted, could hardly stand on his own two legs. It was apparent that he desperately needed some support. He, thus, leaned trustingly on Babatunde's arm. However, Babatunde, when certain that Obinna had leaned completely on him, suddenly grabbed Obinna cruelly by the hand, and thrust him with a violent force into the gory valley of destruction below with a boisterous laughter…

Obinna woke up instantly and sat up in his bed, shaking terribly in every limb. He was sweating profusely. His heart was beating rapidly, his facial muscles were twitching haphazardly, and his breathing was severely laboured. He coughed violently, rubbed his eyes, looked around him, recognized his room and realized he had been dreaming.

"Oh, it was all a nightmare," he said dreamily, "What a terribly frightening one! Was that a vision of an impending doom, or of the end of the world?"

He stood up still trembling, staggered to the kitchen, opened the refrigerator and took a long drink of cold water. When his mind became clearer, and his nerves steadier, he started reflecting on the dream he just had. Though it was only two o'clock in the morning, Obinna lay wide-awake in bed and was too agitated to go back to sleep. Was the dream trying to warn him of something, of a looming danger for instance? Could it ever be possible that a very kind and wonderful friend like Babatunde, whom he had grown to love and trust so sincerely, ever hurt him let alone kill him as Babatunde had done in the dream? These were the questions Obinna was asking himself. However, after arguing with himself for a while, he felt certain that Babatunde could never hurt him.

"Babatunde is just too good to hurt anyone," he reassured himself in a loud voice.

As though to counter the conclusion he had reached about Babatunde, a clear picture of how Babatunde had plunged him so recklessly and so wickedly to his death in the dream flitted rapidly through his mind. However, Obinna quickly dismissed it. He told himself repeatedly that it was just a dream, and not the reality.

"What are dreams anyway?" He asked himself thoughtfully, "Are dreams not just tricks played on us by our own consciousness through a not-so-ordered rearrangement of the sensory impressions stored in our memory, even those impressions we had as early as the time of our conception in the womb? Certainly, all these impressions stored in our memory are capable of undergoing rearrangement and manifest as dreams during sleep."

He reminded and assured himself that he was well-versed in these matters and that dreams were really nothing to worry about. Thus, Obinna relegated his dream to a trick played on him by his consciousness, and pushed it completely out of his mind.

II

It appeared Cupid might have shot one of the many arrows from his quiver at Obinna's heart; for after Obinna had set his eyes on Martha, the last time he visited Babatunde's house, he had been unable to get her out of his mind. He thought about her all day long and even at night, as he dreamt frequently of her. Perhaps that arrow was shot at that same moment when their eyes met and locked for a few seconds during the lunch they had in Babatunde's house. Whether his eyes were wide-open, or deeply shut, all he saw were Martha's radiantly beautiful face and form. What charmed him more was Martha's admirable personality. Although Martha did not say much at the table during that lunch, her richly-attractive voice charmed him tremendously. He loved how Martha made the few comments she made at the table, and even more, he loved the sound of her voice. Her voice and personality had aroused something in him, something inexpressible. In addition, Martha's response, when she was rebuked by Juliette for her excessive devotion to

Christianity, deeply impressed him. Rather than exchange words with Juliette, and thus create an unpleasant scene in Babatunde's house, Martha had displayed such a great character by simply walking away without saying as little as a single word in her own defence. He greatly admired women who showed a lot of respect and displayed such strength of character whatever the circumstances might be. However, there seemed to be a huge and an impassable gulf between himself and Martha. Martha was an ardent devotee of the Christian Faith; while he does not believe in any religion or faith. In his own words, "All religions are a scam of the wise to deceive the unwise." How on earth is he ever going to get Martha to embrace his own Philosophy of life, his own absolute lack of faith in all religions, especially in Christianity? He does not know how, but he believed there must be a way, and he was determined to find it. At this point, he remembered Dr. Maria Onwuka-Smith's, "Middle Path Philosophy." But he was not sure he was ready to embrace a middle path in religious issues, not after what he thought he knew about all religions.

"No," he said to himself aloud, "I cannot set my beliefs aside, not even slightly, certainly not after the truth that I have found out about religions."

Nevertheless, in spite of this seemingly-insurmountable obstacle, Obinna was hopeful, and remained obsessed with Martha. It got to a point, this obsession drove him to call Babatunde on the telephone, and after the exchange of pleasantries, he nicely but bashfully demanded for Martha's phone number from Babatunde. Babatunde seemed amused and chuckled quietly to himself. He responded that he does not have Martha's phone number. However, he informed him that Juliette had the number, and that he would hand his phone over to Juliette so that she could tell him the number. Obinna soon heard Juliette's high pitched voice on the telephone, and they both greeted. Thereafter, Juliette suddenly laughed because she knew instantly that Obinna was smitten. She could recognize the signs. Then she called out the digits of Martha's phone number to him; she seemed to know the number by heart. Then she added playfully, and with a soft laughter:

"Please, Mr. Obinna, I'll really appreciate it if you can bring Martha out of her shell. She has created a self-made shell around herself, that, she is now living in a virtual prison. You will indeed be doing me a great favour if you can help to bring her out of this prison because I love Martha so much. I still consider her my best friend though she walked out on me the other day when we were having lunch together."

"I apologize for her behaviour that day," he responded, "I'll see what I can do to make her change. Thank you very much for the number."

"You're welcome anytime, Mr. Obinna, and good luck with her," Juliette concluded with a giggle.

III

Few weeks later, Obinna left his old apartment and moved into a new, two bedroom apartment in the Surulere area of Lagos. The apartment, though small, was lovely and tidy. It was situated in a middle-class section of the city, and Obinna had taken pains to furnish the apartment tastefully. He had acquired some of the basic necessities he had always wanted, necessities that he felt made life worth more living, things like: a television set, a laptop computer, refrigerator, nice set of home furniture, new set of fine clothes and shoes. His new neighbourhood, unlike the one he moved away from, was quiet and clean. He also had more than enough cash to feed himself well and cater for his other needs for many months ahead. He had paid a two-year, rent advance for his new apartment; therefore, accommodation would not pose a problem for him in a long time. Indeed Obinna now looked more relaxed, and his appearance had also improved tremendously. He looked more handsome, having added just the right amount of weight.

THE PACT

The once prominent hollows on his face had all disappeared, and his face now had more flesh and a fresh look. A good number of his hairs—many of which had turned prematurely grey because of inadequate nourishment and hardship—had reverted virtually to their natural dark colour. Being naturally blessed with lush hair growth, Obinna's hair now stood thickly compacted on his head, having lost their previous fluffiness. He had also lost his brooding and morose look; but rather now appeared friendly and optimistic.

However, he was still bothered by the fact that he does not have a job. Up till the present moment, he has been living well on the goodwill of his friend, Joshua Anjorin Babatunde. He knew he could not continue to depend on Babatunde for the rest of his life. He wanted to work for Babatunde, and had asked Babatunde to find an appropriate position for him in any of his businesses, perhaps as Business Manager. He had boasted of his theoretical knowledge of Business to Babatunde, a knowledge, which he averred, was extraordinary. Why, he had made an excellent grade in Business Administration, one of the courses he took in the University. He told Babatunde he would bring that knowledge to bear in managing his business empire. However, Obinna was astounded—chilled to the marrow—when Babatunde responded dispassionately that he owned no businesses. When Obinna recovered from his shock, he wondered with intensity how Babatunde had made his enormous wealth, a wealth that seemed inexhaustible. Instantly, like a curious cat, he was tempted to ask Babatunde about the source of his wealth, but stopped himself just before the words escaped from his mouth. He was a little disturbed that there was a part of Babatunde, his beloved friend and benefactor, which seemed shrouded in mystery, a part that he could not possibly trust. He had asked himself severally if Babatunde was involved in some form of fraudulent activity like drugs, or crime. Without any inkling to the answer, he merely told himself that Babatunde was just too good a man to be involved in any kind of fraudulent activity. Then he tried to convince himself that perhaps Babatunde was fortunate enough to have inherited a huge amount of fortune. Nonetheless, in order to satisfy his curiosity, he told himself that he would ask Babatunde how his money was made, perhaps not immediately, but he was certain he would ask him in the near future. He would let Babatunde know that he, Obinna, was more or less like a brother to him, and that Babatunde should seal their bond of brotherhood and friendship by showing him the way to wealth and independence. He would let Babatunde know that he does not wish to be as wealthy as Babatunde, but just wealthy enough to lead a good and respectable life. Strangely enough, he felt certain that Babatunde would be willing to share his secret of wealth with him once he posed the question.

"In the interim," he addressed himself aloud; thus breaking his reverie, "I'll continue to fill out applications and attend job interviews as I have been doing now for almost twenty years."

Chapter 7

The gorgeous Saint Christopher's Cathedral, a gigantic nine story edifice, situated in the highly commercialized Lagos Island, was a monumental reminder of how religious Lagosians are. Its four magnificent towers extend far upwards and finally appear to penetrate the sky when viewed from the ground level. Its various attractively-cultivated shrubs and evergreen trees gave the Cathedral an excellent shade from the sun, and offered an additional cover for the worshippers on occasions when the Cathedral was filled to overflowing. A variety of birds—pigeons, canaries, robins and bluebirds—built their nests on the branches of these trees whose fruits and seeds also provided abundant nourishing food for the birds. Many of these birds could be seen flocking in large numbers, especially on Sundays, around the Cathedral—each one enthusiastically singing its own tuneful song, as though praising and thanking God for the shelter and wholesome nourishment from the trees. The Cathedral had the capacity to accommodate up to twenty thousand Parishioners who converge there to celebrate Mass every Sunday. Although Mass was celebrated everyday; it was only on Sundays and during special ceremonies that the Cathedral was usually filled to capacity and beyond. It had five main entrances and exit points. There were three excellently-decorated altars each aligned to the north, northeast and northwest directions. The pews were made of brilliantly-polished acacia wood, cushioned, and were also aligned almost perfectly in the same directions with each of the altars. Towering superbly above each of the altar was a gigantic Crucifix, an emblem of the Catholic Church. On the face of the Christ crucified, even as He hung sorrowfully on the

Cross of Suffering, was a faint smile, a smile which silently proclaim *Forgiveness of sins and Life everlasting* for all of humanity that believe in Him. Magnificent larger-than-life paintings of the Stations of the Cross and of the Saints richly embellished the walls of the Cathedral. The interior of the Cathedral was of a golden hue: its roof was extensively decorated, Gothic style and architecture, and seemed to be cast entirely in solid gold. The edges of its massive windows were lined with gold, all its giant candlestands on the smooth floor, and the ones positioned upon the altars, were all made of solid gold. The paintings of the Stations of the Cross, and of the Saints, were all set on golden canvas; the Chalice, Patens, Ciboria, Censers and each of the Crucifix were all made of pure, solid gold.

It was a Saturday morning, and Mass was in progress but attended only sparingly, less than a thousand Parishioners were in attendance in the huge Cathedral. Seated at the eastern wing of the Cathedral was the beautiful young woman, Martha, in a deep, devotional attitude.

The Church Organ came alive and the *Sanctus* rang out, the congregation sang aloud:

> "Holy, Holy, Holy
> Lord God of hosts,
> Heaven and earth are
> full of Your glory.
> Hosanna in the highest.
> Blessed is He who comes
> in the name of the Lord.
> Hosanna in the highest."

The entire Cathedral vibrated with the highly melodious *Sanctus*; and even the numerous birds outside the Cathedral seemed to pick up the vibration and echo it very loudly and sweetly amongst themselves—from one to the other—as though to add their own voices to the praise of the *Lord God of Hosts* and thus make up for the insufficiently attended Mass.

After the Communion rites, the officiating Priest concludes the Mass by blessing the people saying:

"May the Almighty
God bless you:
the Father, the Son, and
the Holy Spirit. The Mass
is ended, go forth in peace
and announce the Gospel
of our Lord Jesus Christ!"

The Parishioners began to leave the Cathedral through the various exit routes, and Martha, using one of the eastern exits, was soon standing outside, greeting and shaking hands with some of the people she knew.

"Sister Martha! Sister Martha!" cried a voice behind her.

Martha turned around swiftly, and saw a middle-aged woman in the garb of a Nun approaching her steadily. Martha smiled the instant she saw her. The Nun, Sis. Morenike Oluwaseun, was the Abbess of the Franciscan Convent situated in the outskirts of Lagos Island, not very far from the Cathedral. The moment she reached where Martha stood, both women embraced.

"Why, Abbess Morenike Oluwaseun," Martha addressed the Nun as they broke the embrace, "So nice to see you. I was just thinking of you now as I intend to pay a visit to the Convent today."

"Martha," said the Nun breathlessly, "You won't believe what happened. Sister Philippa made away with the Church offerings—all the offerings collected over several months—kept specifically for the upkeep of the poor."

Martha was utterly flabbergasted.

"How awfully sacrilegious!" She exclaimed, "What in the world could have come over such a seemingly nice religious woman, and cause her to cast her Christian tenets so recklessly aside and behave so unwholesomely?"

"Well," the Nun responded, "We knew she had financial challenges, and that she was solely responsible for the care of her younger siblings."

"But Abbess," Martha interjected calmly, "That doesn't make it right."

"Yes, Martha, you're right. It doesn't make it right in the eyes of God," the Nun responded, "Want, or poverty, should never be used as an excuse for stealing. That is absolutely unacceptable. A visit had been paid to her residence on three occasions by some of the top Church officials, and none of her siblings—all supposedly Church members—would disclose her whereabouts or give any useful information about her. And you know the Church would never recourse to the use of force, so the Church is letting it lie."

"Oh, what a bad decision made by Sister Philippa," Martha said with a disturbed expression on her face, "It never pays to spoil one's reputation because of gold. Perhaps all Sister Philippa needed to have done was to talk to somebody about her challenges; someone might have been able to help her out of her difficulties, or at least, ameliorate them, and she need not have committed such a shameful act."

"Remember," said the Nun, "In the Gospels of our Lord Jesus Christ, it is clearly stated that we should ask in order to receive; to seek in order to find, with all certitude. The truth of the Gospels had been proven too many times to count, but it seems many of us who have been in the Church for long are yet to learn that basic truth."

As the ladies conversed; suddenly, a little golden-feathered canary flew swiftly towards Martha, circled around her head three times, then perched gently on her right shoulder singing a very beautiful tune as it settled.

"Do not drive it away! Do not drive it away!" Cried the Nun… "Let it relax on your shoulder for it has found good rest there; and something—I know not what—must have singled you out for its notice among all the Worshippers present here."

Martha, with head turned to her right shoulder, watched the canary quietly amused, chuckling several times to herself.

"How are you, little bird?" She said to the canary after a while, "And how is your mommy? Be sure to say hello to your mommy for me."

As though in response, the little bird nodded quietly and changed its song to a more beautiful tune, nodded again, and suddenly took flight from Martha's shoulder. Martha laughed softly as the bird took off.

"Goodbye little bird," she said as the bird flew away still singing.

"Do not laugh it off as just another chance occurrence," said the Nun, "That was a lovely and spectacular sight. You know not what untold blessings that bird has brought to you."

Martha, still smiling, looked ahead and saw Rev. Fr. John Michaels followed by three men, carrying some religious articles in a bag, walking towards them. Rev. Fr. John Michaels was the most senior Parish Priest and Pastor of the Cathedral. He was a balding and tanned sixty-five year old Northern Irish by birth, but naturalized Nigerian having spent a large part of his life in the country. He initially came into the Country as a Catholic Missionary, but fell in love with the country and the peculiarities of the intensely diverse cultures of its people, and eventually decided to settle down, work and live permanently in the country. He was a tall, jolly and good-looking fellow with a slightly fleshy face. He had two deep furrows on his forehead, and faint ones at both corners of his mouth. His area of special interest was Exorcism; and had trained, studied, and researched extensively on the subject. He was reputed to have exorcised and liberated over a thousand persons whose Souls were supposedly chained and oppressed by the devil. He was far more famed as an Exorcist than as a Catholic Priest, and his fame extends far and wide beyond the shores of Nigeria. He had performed exceptionally difficult exorcism in his native Northern Ireland as well as in South America and many countries in Europe. He achieved excellent results in every occasion.

"I'm yet to encounter any accursed demon of hell that I'm unable to cast out." He would say very proudly to himself. And because of this reputation of his, he enjoyed unusual respect and admiration from everyone who knew him.

Martha and the Nun bowed respectfully as the highly revered Priest and his entourage reached where they stood.

"How are you, Abbess Oluwaseun and you, Sister Martha?" He asked them with a smile.

"We are fine and blessed, Father," replied both ladies.

Rev. Fr. Michaels, still in his cassocks, told the ladies he was on his way out to see a member of the laity who was very ill and believed to be possessed by demons. He wanted to go and pray with the sick man, exorcise his demons and liberate him from the shackles of demoniac possession. After the exchange of pleasantries, the Priest pronounced a benediction on the ladies and departed with his entourage.

"What an exceptionally-gifted man," noted Martha as the Priest and his three followers continued on their way, "To be so imbued with divine power as to be able to exorcise devils and heal the sick, even as Christ Himself did, is a reflection of how beloved Rev. Fr. Michaels is to God."

"He is undoubtedly beloved of the Most High God" agreed the Nun, "Eh…en" said the Nun prodding Martha slightly with her hand,

and resuming their previous discussion before Rev. Fr. Michaels interrupted them. "The implication of Sister Philippa's unruly action," the Nun resumed, "Is that none of the five Orphanages under the care of our Cathedral can get anything from the Church any time soon. Things will become much tougher and uglier for those poor orphans, some of them will probably starve, and many will have to drop out of school except the Church figures out a way to raise the money very quickly for them."

"How terrible!" Martha, visibly disturbed, responded with misty eyes, "How much exactly did Sister Philippa make away with?"

"Four hundred and thirty-five thousand naira," replied the Nun.

Martha, still looking very disturbed, stared blankly into space for a few moments.

"Those poor orphans do not have to suffer so badly because of the thoughtless action of one person," she said meditatively with the usual pathos in her voice, "Please, dear Abbess," she said to the Nun, "Come with me to my car.

I will go with you to the Convent, I have some items I want to present to the ladies there, and I'll write out a cheque of four hundred thousand naira to you for the orphans. And please, Abbess, I don't want my name announced in Church as the benefactor of the orphans. If asked, just tell the Priest that the donor prefers anonymity."

The Nun was completely astounded and deeply moved by Martha's magnanimity that she was speechless momentarily.

"May God bless you, my daughter; may God bless you, my daughter," She said repeatedly. These were the only words she could utter to express her gratitude to Martha for her philanthropic gesture.

The two women walked to the parking lot, and both entered Martha's *Hyundai Elantra*. The Abbess sat next to Martha on the passenger seat; the back seat and boot of the vehicle were already loaded with various gift items Martha wanted to present to the Nuns in the Convent. Martha opened the glove compartment of her car, took out the cheque book she usually kept there, filled and signed it, then tore it out and handed the cheque over to the Abbess. This action was followed by the pronouncement of more benedictions upon Martha. Thereafter, she started the engine of the car, reversed, and slowly left the premises of the Cathedral; later accelerating and gaining momentum gradually as it made its way to the Convent.

CHAPTER 8

"Religion is a scam of the wise to deceive the unwise!" Obinna declared, openly, with heat and energy, in Babatunde's house with Babatunde in rapt attention. Both men were seated conversing together in one of Babatunde's magnificently furnished living rooms and had drunk several bottles of strong, alcoholic wine after a hearty repast. Obinna had paid a visit to Babatunde's house, on invitation by Babatunde, who felt a little lonely, and needed company and someone to talk with. Juliette, Babatunde's fiancée and closest companion, had travelled abroad to do her usual monthly shopping, and was expected back in two weeks. Babatunde sat with an air of royalty on an exalted seat that looked more like a throne, or cathedra, on an elevated platform in the living room. And together with his loose, flowing, shiny garments which covered his entire body except for his head, hands and feet, he had the unmistakable appearance of a king or an emperor except for the absence of a staff of authority in his hand. On the other hand, Obinna sat on a seat below the platform where Babatunde sat, and with his sweatshirt and jeans, Obinna was in the attitude of a subject to a sovereign ruler.

"I did a very intensive, background check on most Heads of Churches or 'General Overseers,' as they loved to be addressed these days," Obinna said, "And found out that many of them had gone into religion specifically to make money. Most of them were very poor, stupid, wretched jackasses without jobs or any means of livelihood who were forced into religion by desperate Want. They were never called to serve, as most of them claimed, into what was meant to be a totally selfless and divine calling. And because Christianity is more or less like an organized crime these days, it has completely failed the people. However, since man is inherently religious by nature—always seeking a supernatural 'something' to cast the crushing weight of his seemingly endless troubles upon—he feels the compulsion to keep attending Church regularly in spite of its abysmal failure. The number of Churches in Lagos for instance is increasing in geometric progression but so is crime and corruption in all ramifications. A small street, in a typical Nigerian city, for instance, can boast of at least one or more Churches, but the members are totally bereft of the morals and spiritual values the Churches are supposed to be teaching or instilling into them. The greatest frauds and corruption in our society are perpetrated by seemingly decent, Church-attending and highly-religious people many of whom actually occupy positions of authority in their various Churches. Investigate the Public Service of our country, and you will be astonished to find that the most corrupt officials are often the ones who embrace religion the most, some of them actually doing Thanksgiving, shamelessly, and without even the slightest prick of conscience, in their Churches after every successful steal in office. It appeared that the Churches, or more specifically, the Clergy, in reality, encouraged these public Officials to steal by consistently focusing on materialism and prosperity as the theme of most of their sermons. The Church literally tells its members: 'Get rich at all expense, even at the expense of the Planet, if that is what it takes to get rich, then bring the money to Church!' What an absurdity! If you are rich, the Church lavishes you with endless praises, shows you utmost respect; but if you are poor, the Church can hardly contain its irritation with you, and treats you with profoundly demeaning disdain. I know that there are some Churches here, in this very city, where what qualifies you as member is the size of your bank account, or your status in society. There are, yet, others where pitiful segregation exists in the Church;

where the poor and the rich are not permitted to sit in the same section of the Church!"

Babatunde, who was naturally taciturn, listened attentively but said nothing. He sat on his magnificent chair like a powerful monarch would sit on his throne without a care in the world. From time to time, he sipped his wine, refilled his glass when empty, and continued to listen to Obinna. However, the whimsical smile on his face, the constant nod of his head from his exalted throne-like chair, were indications that he was in full agreement with Obinna's vituperations and callous denigration of religions—Christianity specifically.

"I know a Church in Obalende," resumed Obinna, "Its weekly collections were meagre, so its Pastor came up with a bright idea of how to squeeze more money out of its members by insisting that the members bring out their offerings and display them openly by holding up the offerings with both hands, high above their heads, with the notes fully stretched out for everyone in the Church to see; ostensibly to invoke the blessings of God upon the offerings. Consequently, the Church members, most of whom were used to giving only five, ten, or twenty naira as offering felt too ashamed to display such niggardly sums above their heads, and started donating from five hundred naira and above, albeit reluctantly. The result? Church offerings soared tremendously and increased by over one thousand percent. Thereafter, the Pastor started smiling very happily to the Bank every week!"

At this point Babatunde couldn't contain himself any longer. He suddenly bursts into a fit of strident laughter. Rarely was he ever moved to this type of humour by any circumstance.

"And what about God?" He asked after his prolonged laughter, "Why is He just sitting up there in His so called heaven and doing nothing about all the evils that had been wrought in His Name... all the evils that are still being committed with impunity everyday, by scoundrels, with religion as reason and excuse?"

"Because there is no such being as an all-powerful God existing anywhere in the skies!" replied Obinna with derision. Then he added with egotistic pride, "There is no heaven and there is no God!"

From his exalted seat, Babatunde smiled at Obinna. His face brightened with intensity as he nodded his head apparently in agreement with Obinna, and wanted to hear more of the blasphemous utterances of this enigmatic being he had made his close friend and ally.

"Or, if He does exists," continued Obinna, "Then He simply does not care a jot about what it is claimed He created—the world and all its inhabitants—mankind especially. How could there possibly be a God in a world where evil triumphs so outstandingly over good? Consider the hunger and starvation in the world? Consider all the vicious terrorist organizations that have spread across the Globe like the tentacles of an octopus, organizations that take so much pleasure in slaughtering innocent people, so recklessly, in the world today. If God is up there somewhere in the skies, why hasn't He, or why didn't He do anything about the ceaseless and wanton bloodshed? Or He must be cruel, if He exists at all, to observe all the ills of the world and then turn quietly away or veil His face from humanity that so desperately need Him. Consider also the millions of people who perished so miserably at the two world wars; wars where innumerable innocent and seemingly good people were swept away with the outrightly wicked ones, and God allowed that to happen? The world's most talented scientists have travelled to Space several times; some of them looked out specifically for God, and could not find Him anywhere in that vast emptiness known as Space."

"I agree absolutely with you," said Babatunde rapturously, with a smile, his eyes seemingly transfixed downwards on Obinna's face. Then he poured himself another glass of the fine wine, emptying what was their sixth bottle of the strong alcoholic drink that evening, and swallowed it all in one gulp.

"Consider the unfair segregation in all human societies," Obinna said, "Some people were born into staggering wealth while others, through no fault of theirs, were born into direst poverty, and had to struggle, scratch and claw at every point in their lives to put even a small morsel of food in their mouths. Some children were born into this world, through no fault of theirs, with crippling or debilitating diseases that impaired their survival chances and their chances of competing fairly in today's economically oriented world. How could God, if He actually exists, allow all such appalling things to happen? I, personally, concluded a long time ago that an omnipotent, omnipresent and omniscient God—as presented by the Clergy—doesn't exist anywhere; either here on earth or anywhere else in the skies. I believe man simply creates a god big enough, in his own heart, that take care of his problems, that is all. Even those who espouse religion so enthusiastically today know in their heart of hearts that what I have just said is the absolute truth, but out of fear of being labelled unbelievers or atheists, would not want to acknowledge the truth. Religion is considered today by many simply as a social activity and nothing more. Many attend Church today, not out of a sense of belief or devotion to God, but simply out of the sense of fulfilling a social obligation. Today, the majority of people consider Church attendance as an opportunity to see old friends or make new ones, show off their wealth or clothes, and possibly as a place to meet their future or life partners. That is why the Church has failed so woefully as a moulder of characters, an instructor of morals, and a shaper of destinies."

"Once again, I agree completely with everything you have said, Obinna." Babatunde said after Obinna had paused from his outrageous profanities. "What impressed me more," Babatunde said, "Is the courage you have shown in studying, arriving, and speaking so freely about your convictions because I know that everything you have said is bursting at the seams with the truth. I absolutely hold the same views with you in matters of religion, Obinna. But what are your views about the Soul, Obinna?" Babatunde asked in an earnest voice as he continued, "The Clergy teaches that every human being is endowed with a Soul that survives the death of the body. The Soul is supposedly immortal and goes either up to heaven or down to hell, depending on the kind of life lived, after the death of the body it animated. What do you make of the Soul, Obinna?"

"Balderdash!" replied Obinna, "Absolute nonsense!" He suddenly laughed out disdainfully, and said: "I'm really surprised at you, Babatunde, for asking about the Soul! Don't tell me you believe in the Soul, or I'll laugh you to scorn right now! No Scientist has been able to prove, by any scientific means or by any other means, the existence of anything called the Soul. And I tell you that many Scientists have made huge attempts. My philosophy teaches that the Soul is just another big lie of the Clergy! Life begins at conception, and terminates instantly at death. That is the absolute truth, Babatunde!"

Babatunde did not respond, but merely nodded his head and smiled—his mute sign of assent.

"And just as mankind had been deceived into believing in the existence of an omnipotent God by the crafty and irresponsible Clergy…" resumed Obinna, "Thus had he been led, so subtly, by the same cunning Clergy into believing in the eternal spirit of evil known as Satan, or the Devil."

Babatunde looked up and laughed discordantly at Obinna's assertions about the devil but said nothing further.

"As a matter of fact," Obinna resumed his vile speech, "All things in the universe are constituted in opposites: Light and Darkness; Male and Female; Hot and Cold; and the list is endless… therefore, if there is a God who represents love and goodness, then there must be a devil that represents hate and evil, so the Clergy reasoned. Therefore, it became absolutely necessary for the Clergy to create the concept of the devil to take responsibility for man's atrocities. In reality, all things perceived or seen as evil today were perpetrated by man, and man alone, against his fellow man. And as for natural disasters, they are the results of man's negligence of how to take care of his environment, the results of his constant abuse of the planet. However, because man is apt to shift the blames of his wrongdoings, which he so justly deserved, elsewhere; the poor, old, and non-existent devil had thus been accused of far more blames and evils than he truly deserved were he to be really in existence."

He stopped abruptly here. Babatunde who had been listening to him attentively did not volunteer any response this time, but appeared to be busy with his own thoughts with an expressionless face. As the silence became more awkwardly prolonged, Babatunde, still maintaining his silence, shifted a little in his throne-like seat and impulsively rang the bell affixed to his throne-chair. A servant appeared instantly. He asked for more whisky and the servant left immediately for the wine cabinet, collected the whisky, the seventh one, uncorked it, and refilled both men's glasses.

Obinna, already tipsy, picked up his glass and swallowed a mouthful of the whisky then replaced the glass on the table. He grimaced as the whisky scorched his intestines the instant he swallowed it.

"Babatunde," he said, "You have been such an excellent friend to me, exceeding all men I have known in the past in acts of generosity and kindness. I know I also owe my life to you, and that I have lived well on your generosity for several months now. My indebtedness to you cannot be quantified in words. For everything you've done for me, I'm indeed exceedingly grateful to you. But please, Babatunde, remember this old adage of our people: 'Don't give me fish; but teach me how to fish, and you would have made me a better and independent person for life.' Please, don't think me importunate or impudent because I knew that I asked you for a job, not long ago, and you replied that you don't have any job to offer me."

He paused a little here to study Babatunde's face which remained expressionless. Unable to read any meaning on Babatunde's face, he continued, but this time, somewhat half-heartedly.

"Apparently," he said, "You don't do any work yourself, Babatunde; but your wealth seemed to have no limits or bounds. How did you manage to gain and stay so wealthy without having to use your hands or brain to work, Babatunde? As your friend and brother veritably—to use the same phrase you used to address me that night at Tasty treats Restaurant—please, kindly share the secret of your enormous wealth with me so that I can be wealthy too, and will not have to be dependent on you for the rest of my life. I promise that I shall forever be loyal and grateful to you."

Babatunde still remained silent on his exalted chair but was staring into space. About five minutes after Obinna's plea; a soft smile slowly lit up his face, and he looked downwards at Obinna, straight and full, in the eye, and said in a deeply-cold, warning accent:

"Obinna, why are you trying to find out the source of my wealth?" Without waiting for a reply, he continued, "I have tried to be very liberal with you, gave my undying friendship to you, saved you from a certain death, gave you sufficient cash to clean you up—transforming you from the destitute you were when I first met you—to the new corporate-looking guy you are today. I also made sure you don't lack cash at any point in time, keeping you well-supplied with more than enough. I further encouraged you to leave your old apartment—a 'rat hole' by every standard—for the more decent and suitable one you now occupy. My next plan is to buy you a new and befitting car very soon. What do you still want and why are you not satisfied, Obinna?"

"Oh, no, please, Babatunde, don't misunderstand me," began Obinna apologetically, but he was silenced instantly by an authoritative gesture from Babatunde.

"For your own good, Obinna," Babatunde resumed, "And for mine, I don't think you want to know where my wealth comes from. I think it is better you remain ignorant of the source of my wealth, at least for the time being! Perhaps in the future, when I'm convinced you are ready, the knowledge you seek now shall be made freely yours, but not before you are ready. I don't think you're ready yet, Obinna. Now, if you don't mind, Obinna, let us proceed to the dining room for supper."

The two men got up and made their way to the massive dining room where another tasty banquet had been prepared by Babatunde's excellent chefs. Twilight approached soon after supper and Obinna took his leave from Babatunde's house. During the supper, both men had conversed very freely as though a little friction had not occurred between them when Obinna pleaded to be privy to Babatunde's secret of wealth. As usual, after supper,

THE PACT

Babatunde had gracefully instructed one of his servants to chauffeur Obinna off in one of his cars to Obinna's residence in Surulere. The servant had also given a large, bulky, brown envelope—a gift from Babatunde—to Obinna as he alighted from the car. He thanked the driver who instantly drove away.

It was already nightfall when Obinna reached his apartment, and his mind was very busy as he walked through the gate of the house. How mysterious Babatunde seemed when he asked him about his wealth.

"What secret could Babatunde be hiding that had given him all his wealth?" Obinna asked himself as he walked down to his apartment.

If anything, Babatunde's hesitancy in sharing this secret had aroused Obinna's curiosity the more that he resolved he was going to ask Babatunde the same question again as soon as another opportunity came. And what did Babatunde mean when he said to him: "Perhaps in the future, when I'm convinced you are ready, the knowledge you seek now shall be made freely yours, but not before you are ready."

"If there is anything I'm ready for in this world right now, it is how to become super wealthy," Obinna mused. "I've been poor for too long. Yes, I am very ready now." He told himself repeatedly, "And I'm going to ask you, Joshua Anjorin Babatunde, this same question again no matter how many times you try to dissuade me with your weird way of talking," he soliloquized.

He felt the envelope that was handed to him by Babatunde's chauffeur, looked inside, and saw many rolls of crispy five hundred naira notes. He estimated that there must be up to one million naira in that envelope as Babatunde had given him the same amount on three occasions in the past. He smiled to himself. He loved the money; at least there was no question about Babatunde's generosity towards him. But what was worrying him was the mystery Babatunde was keeping about how the wealth was made. But he liked the money, and he smiled to himself again. He walked past the gate into the poorly-lit compound, and headed straight for his apartment.

"Hello sweetheart, how are you doing?" A sweet feminine voice said to him from the darkness as he was about to open the door.

Obinna peered into the semidarkness and saw the shape of a smartly-dressed, young lady. On looking closer, he recognized her instantly. It was Monica, his former girlfriend, who walked out of his life almost two years ago.

"Why, Monica!" He said, somewhat surprised, "What on earth are you doing here? And how did you find me here?"

"I visited your former apartment," Monica replied sweetly, "The one we shared together, and met the landlord, Mr. Fatai Johnson. He gave me the directions to this place."

"Mr. Johnson?" cried Obinna, "I can't recall giving my address to that miserable and rascally old man."

"You've changed a lot!" Monica cried excitedly, "You are now looking far more handsome than ever. What miracle happened to you, Obinna? Got a job at last?"

"Honestly, Monica," Obinna said, ignoring her remarks, "I don't remember giving my address to Mr Johnson, that man could...,"

"Forget about Mr. Johnson!" Monica interposed in a loud voice.

She jumped happily into his arms, and kissed him on the lips.

"I missed you," she said.

"How could you possibly miss me when you walked out deliberately on me two years ago?" He asked her.

"I'm very sorry I did that to you," she replied, "But I could no longer tolerate the endless lack of money and of virtually everything necessary to make a relationship work, I just had to move on."

"So, why are you here now?" Obinna asked somewhat angrily.

"Don't be a naughty boy, Obinna. Aren't you pleased to see me?"

Obinna did not answer. He merely tightened his grip over the brown envelope he held in his left hand as though he feared she would snatch the envelope from him and disappear with the money in an instant. Then he started unlocking the door of his apartment.

"Your friend, Halima, passed away last year," he told her.

"Oh, poor Halima!" She exclaimed, "No wonder she no longer returns my calls."

Obinna opened the door of his apartment, stepped inside the dark living room with Monica following behind.

"Halima died a few days later from the complications of having an abortion." Obinna said to her.

"Oh, what a poor girl—just twenty-six years—may her Soul rest in peace," responded Monica.

Obinna searched for the light switch in the darkness, found it, and switched it on. The entire living room lit up instantly with a bright white glow from the powerful electric bulb in the ceiling.

"What a plush apartment!" Monica cried, her face, very joyful. "Everything here is squeaky-clean, Obinna, your apartment is literally glittering with money!"

He did not answer.

"Please, sit down," he said, "Excuse me for two minutes, I'll be right back."

He disappeared into his bedroom, and quickly hid the envelope beneath his bed, then returned to find Monica still admiring his living room. Monica was tall, slim, and attractively built. Her hair was very nicely done, and it still had a fresh-smell. She was very pretty and desirable without necessarily being beautiful.

She looked up, saw Obinna entered, and smiled at him flirtatiously.

"Obinna, sweetheart," she said, "You've been doing very well apparently for yourself now. Wow, see how good you're now looking!" she told him with a look of admiration in her eyes, "And your apartment; it is simply awesome."

"Thank you," muttered Obinna.

"It almost seemed as if immediately I left you, your luck turned around, Obinna dear, was that what happened?" She asked with a sudden curious note in her voice.

"Certainly," came the unkind reply from Obinna.

Monica said nothing further but sat down quietly on a sofa, and looked up inquiringly into his eyes.

"So what brought you here, Monica?" He asked somewhat sternly.

"Nothing really," came the reply from Monica, "I guess I was suffering from a prick of conscience. It was unfair the way I just walked away from you, I guess I only wanted to see your face again, perhaps for the last time."

"Why for the last time?" Obinna queried.

"Well, not long after I left you," began Monica, "I met this rich and nice sixty-two year old widower who needed a wife and companion. We dated for a few months, and later, he proposed to me. I had no other choice; so, I accepted his proposal."

"What!" Obinna cried, "You accepted to marry a sixty-two year old man? That's almost twice your age, Monica!"

"I know; I know..." she said repeatedly, "But I had no choices, and I'm not getting any younger either, I'm now thirty-two years old, Obinna."

"I think I know the real reason why you accepted to marry him," Obinna said in a very firm manner, "It was because of his money and nothing else! I know you very well, Monica. All your decisions are always influenced by money, which was why you left me in the first place! You left me, Monica, because I didn't have any money then!"

"Please, please, Obinna, be gentle with me," Monica pleaded, her eyes becoming misty. "I know that I wronged you very badly by leaving you the way I did; but the circumstances around you then were unbearable, and in that state, you couldn't have been able to support a wife anyway."

She suddenly stood up from the sofa, tears dripping from her eyes, and with outstretched arms, she approached Obinna and looked straight into his eyes.

"Dearest, Obinna." She addressed him when she was within arm's length from him, "I still love you very much. I can still disengage from him and call off the wedding if you are willing to accept me back, please."

Obinna laughed suddenly in her face—a wild discordant laughter—and yelled very loudly:

"Impossible!" He continued in a loud voice, "A dog does not return to its own vomit! Monica, you vomited me out of your guts; and your vomitus, I choose to remain!"

After several more pleas amidst freely falling tears from Monica were repeatedly rebuffed by Obinna, she sank back hopelessly into the sofa sobbing quietly with her face hidden between her hands, a very pathetic picture of a woman who had loved and lost. After about thirty minutes without any further exchange of words between the twain, the wall clock, as if in protest to the uncomfortable silence, chimed the hour of eleven o'clock loudly.

"It is getting very late, Monica," Obinna told her quietly. "I think it is time you take your leave before it gets too late."

Monica, whose face was still covered by both hands, looked up slowly at Obinna. Her face was pretty and expressionless; her eyes were still a little red from the tears which she wiped slowly away.

"Obinna," she said very quietly, "I don't believe you'll throw me out of your house this night. See how late it is. What if I'm kidnapped out there, or something horrible happens to me? Please, Obinna, I cannot leave tonight."

He looked at her angrily but managed to control himself. He knew there was really nothing he could do to make her leave right away. If anything happened to her, should he force her to leave, he knew he would never be able to forgive himself. After all, this was a woman he had loved dearly before. Out of desperation, he gave up and shrugged his shoulders.

"Okay," he said, "You may stay the night if you wish."

Chapter 9

Obinna's cash quickly gave out and soon found himself in need of money urgently. He tried to call his best friend and benefactor, Joshua Anjorin Babatunde, on the telephone, but could not reach him as Babatunde's phone numbers were all consistently unavailable. When he visited Babatunde's house, and demanded to see him, the Security operatives that had always welcomed and admitted him very nicely into the house, suddenly turned hostile towards him. They refused him admittance in a very unkind manner, and heaped insults upon him, as they turned him back. He looked desperately and wandered aimlessly around for what he could

THE PACT

possibly do to earn some cash quickly as he was nearing starvation, and no one would lend him even a farthing. He received information about a massive construction project going on somewhere in one of the suburbs of Lagos. The company had recently engaged many new hands for work. He decided to try his luck there for a job, and thus, visited the site. It was a colossal construction site. There were ongoing constructions of hundreds of new buildings—hotels, offices and accommodations. It was twilight when Obinna got there and the place was very noisy and poorly lit.

But what did not seem right at the construction site were the numerous taskmasters—whip in hand—set over all the workers at the site. The workers, stripped almost naked except for the rag-like loincloth around their hips, were very hard at work—carrying blocks, digging, moving earth, carrying and mixing cement—the activities were numerous. They were very dirty, stank badly, sweated much and bled profusely. They wailed, loudly and frightfully, as the taskmasters' merciless whips came down heavily upon them, connecting fiercely with their skins, and at times, lifting away a chunk of their skins. Then go the whips again, tracing fiery circles in the air, and descending brutally-hard upon the bodies of the dreadful-looking workers. This continued repeatedly, and was consistently followed by more frightening wailing after wailing.

"What manner of madness is this?" Obinna asked, intensely amazed, on seeing the ugly sight. "This is far worse than what the slave drivers did hundreds of years ago!"

He moved nearer to take a closer look, and instantly, his nose picked up the gut-wrenching stench: the smell of grime, blood and sweat intermingled. But what was more appalling to him were the cries of the workers as the ruthless taskmasters whipped them unceasingly to bloody pulps. Their cries gave him a very creepy feeling—the sound they made, frightfully unearthly—like the cries of lost Souls in perdition. A certain man was singled out by three taskmasters, all of whom stood over the cowering man, and down came their whips, crack after crack, upon the poor Soul till he was completely covered in his own blood. Obinna, on looking very hard, fancied he could recognize the poor victim, and instinctively dashed forward to rescue him from his torturers. As he got close enough, he suddenly stopped as though he had run into an invisible brick wall; feeling suddenly very frightened—for the face of the man being brutalized—was the same as that of his father's. He looked closer to confirm the identity. But, there was no mistaking the identity, it was undoubtedly his father looking exactly the same as Obinna knew him.

"Daddy! Daddy!" He screamed, "What are you doing here…in this place of suffering and misery?"

The man looked up at Obinna from where he lay on the ground in a bloody heap, and beckoned to him. Obinna moved forward, saw the deep anguish in his father's eyes, and also perceived an unuttered warning on his lips—a warning unmistakably for Obinna, but no word escaped from his mouth. One of the taskmasters backing Obinna—the one that seemed more authoritative than the others—raised his whip again with the intent of inflicting more damage on the victim, but Obinna caught his hand in mid-air, dragged the whip away from him, and viciously turned him round, shouting:

"Stop! Do you want to kill him?"

As the taskmaster turned to face him, Obinna shrank back in horror as he recognized the taskmaster's face—it was the face of his friend—the face of Joshua Anjorin Babatunde who suddenly let out a loud frenzied laughter…

Obinna woke up instantly, trembling. He was drenched in sweat in spite of the air conditioner in the room. He was breathing very fast, and his facial muscles were twitching haphazardly. He sat up in his bed, looked beside him, and saw a young woman, fast asleep, lying next to him in the bed. Then everything became clear to him as he recognized Monica and every other object in the neatly-furnished bedroom.

"Another nightmarish dream," he said to himself. "But, why am I always having these bad dreams with Babatunde constantly involved in them?" He asked himself very thoughtfully.

Babatunde seemed a mysterious fellow without a doubt, but he was far nicer and kinder than most men he had ever met. He passed his hand beneath the bed, and groped for the money he had hidden there. The money was still there. So he was not poor again as he seemed in that dream. Why! He could never be as poor as he used to be, having invested some of the money Babatunde had been giving to him wisely in various investments—shares, bonds, mutual funds, and loans—with good interest rates.

"Never again to the extent of not having food to eat," he told himself.

He considered the dream again. This time; his late father, who had been dead for over a decade, featured in the dream, and was being brutally tortured. All these made no sense to him. He reminded himself again that dreams were simply tricks played upon oneself by its own consciousness, and therefore, he pushed it completely out of his mind.

He looked again beside him, and saw the skimpily dressed Monica. She was as lovely as ever in sleep, and appeared to be sleeping very peacefully. His mind went quickly over all the events of the previous night. He realized that he had made a grave mistake by allowing her to stay the night in his apartment.

"I should have been more aggressive with her, and turned her out into the streets however late it was," he said to himself regretfully; for immediately he had given up, and permitted her to stay the night, the old scene had been re-enacted once again with Monica, in profuse tears, resuming her pleas to be accepted back into his life.

He had maintained his stance and refused very sternly. He even told her a lie that he was already engaged to another woman, thinking it would dissuade her from further pleas to be accepted back. But not for Monica who does not care whether or not Obinna was already involved with another woman.

"You must tell her to leave you alone." She had said to him half-pleadingly and half-authoritatively. "You belong to me and to me alone!" In the same tone, she had said, "I was the one who suffered and endured gruelling hardship with you when you had nothing. I was your girlfriend for three heartbreaking years, and now that you are rich, heaven knows I should be the one to enjoy your riches with you; not one strange woman who had no idea where we started from. She cannot just come and reap what she did not sow!" Monica concluded still with the half-authoritative tone in her voice.

"But I don't love you anymore," Obinna had said to her.

"You loved me once," she responded in an aggressive tone, "You will yet learn to love me again."

Then she flung herself recklessly at him, kissing him severally. Obinna tried desperately to restrain her, not sure of her sexual habits in the past two years of her absence from him. But she was very strong, and pressed herself vigorously and persistently upon him. Obinna had lost his guard after a while, and the two had made love passionately; and both had fallen instantly asleep afterwards till he was rudely awakened by the terrifying nightmare.

Obinna took another long look at the half-naked Monica who was still soundly asleep. He saw her beautifully shaped body, the nice hair, the fresh smell from the hair, the nice scent from her body, the smooth curve of her back, down to her legs. All the things he saw suddenly sent a wave of sexual passion surging vigorously through him. However he quickly fought the mounting urge, stifled it, and controlled himself. He told himself that what happened between them the previous night was a mistake. Why, she had literally raped him!

"No doubt that she is very lovely," he said to himself with a frown on his face as he looked away from her. "Looking the way she's looking now, I know some men will gladly part with an arm, or a leg, just to have a go at her. But not me because my heart belongs somewhere else now."

Obinna had been fascinated by Martha, and obsessed with her for some time now. He could not keep her out of his mind, all his thinking was beclouded by thoughts of Martha. He had spoken to Martha on two occasions on the telephone but could not really express himself satisfactorily to her. When he called her the first time, he had carefully described himself to her, prompting her recall of him when they first met at Babatunde's house. Martha seemed excited and remembered clearly meeting him at Babatunde's house a few months ago, and there was exchange of pleasantries between them. To Martha, Obinna's call was just a friendly call, and nothing more. But, when he called her again few weeks later, Martha became curious, not knowing what his reasons for calling her were.

"Would you mind doing me the honour of visiting me at home?" Obinna had asked Martha in a slightly shaky voice on the phone.

Martha, a little surprised, chuckled and responded with the usual pathos in her voice.

"Mr. Obinna," she said, "You must sincerely pardon me as it is not my habit to visit any man at home."

There was a long pause before he responded.

"Alright, Martha," he said, "I understand. But can you have lunch with me at… let's say, 'King-sized Delights' in Ikeja? I know you are very busy, Martha, but let's just spend a little time together and get better acquainted."

Another long pause before Martha responded.

"Where again and when?" She asked eventually.

Obinna could scarcely believe his luck, he feared he was going to be turned down because of Martha's hesitancy and prolonged silence.

"King-sized Delights in Ikeja," he repeated. "It's a nice place. Would Friday evening at 6:00 pm be convenient for you?"

"Alright," she responded after a slight pause, "6:00 pm, Friday evening would be just fine with me."

They both hung up.

He suddenly remembered that his date with Martha was just two days away, and his heart skipped several beats out of anxiety. This could be more complicated now that Monica had literally forced herself back into his life once again. Well, he told himself he had warned Monica that he does not love her anymore, so, whatever happened to her would not be his fault. He was certainly not going to allow Monica come between him and his new heartthrob, Martha. However, at the back of his mind, he knew that even with Martha, nothing was certain as there exists a very wide gulf between them. Martha was a faithful devoted Christian; while he abhorred all Faiths, especially Christianity, with unspeakable revulsion. How he intended to bridge this gulf, he had no idea. He had thought long and hard on the issue but the problem seemed to defy all solutions he had proffered or suggested to himself. However he remained undaunted, and merely said to himself:

"I'll simply sit back, and watch everything unfold sequentially and naturally."

CHAPTER 10

King-sized Delights, a high-class restaurant and entertainment centre where the rich who could afford its numerous pleasures and entertainments came to amuse themselves from time to time, or simply just to while away their time. It was lavishly decorated and furnished with all the modern, state-of-the-art gadgets necessary to meet the ever-increasing demand of the rich for more amusements and entertainments. It had various sections which included a first-class restaurant where all types of local and foreign foods were readily available. Its bars were stock with all exotic and indigenous drinks one could think of, and it never seemed to run out of any. It had a suite of excellent rooms available for those who wished to lodge. There were five, large, well-furnished halls where international conferences could be held. There were also various play sections where young children could play all day without tiring as the options of play seemed endless. Three live bands were always available at every point in time to provide unbroken stream of music to entertain the guests; each band with its own group of dancing, scantily-dressed girls. Its staff consisted mainly of foreign nationals and a few home-grown ones.

It was Friday evening, and the time stood at exactly 6:00 pm. The weekend had already started bustling with activities in the fun-loving city of Lagos as thousands of people, after the close of work, were beginning to flock to the various amusement centres they had chosen to enjoy themselves. King-sized Delights was one of such centres, and the place was already alive with activities for the long weekend.

THE PACT

Seated at one end of the restaurant was Martha, and facing her directly was Obinna. The restaurant was colourfully and romantically lit, and a soft classical music was playing in the background. Where they sat was quieter than the rest of the restaurant, and a conversation could easily be carried on without straining much to hear what was being said. Martha looked exquisitely beautiful; resplendent in her beautiful, colourful blue and red flowery dress. Her shiny hair was packed neatly above her head like the golden crown of an adorable beauty queen. Her fresh, smooth skin dazzled in the colourful light of the restaurant. Her entire aspect was excellently elegant. Obinna was dressed in a black suit, and looked as handsome as ever. He had taken extra care to dress himself up, gazing consistently at his full-length mirror all through the process. Obinna had chosen this expensive place just to impress Martha. However, what he had not taken into consideration was that there was still a group of people, a very rare group, that do not really care very much about some of the very fanciful and glittering things of life. Martha was one of such persons. Had he known her better, and had chosen a far less expensive place, she would not have noticed the difference provided the place was neat and tidy.

"You are absolutely stunning," he said quietly to Martha.

"Thank you very much," Martha responded with a smile, "You look very nice too, much nicer than the last time I saw you in Babatunde's house."

"Oh, that time," moaned Obinna. "I was going through a very stressful situation that was robbing me of my sleep and peace of mind. But it is resolved now,"

"Thank God," Martha responded.

At this point, the waiter brought the ordered food and drinks to the table, and the two of them ate in silence. After eating, the table was cleared, and more drinks were served. Obinna was careful not to order any alcoholic drink as he was bent on making a good impression of himself on Martha.

"So tell me about yourself, Martha." Obinna said.

Martha smiled a little with that childlike innocence that characterized her. Then, very modestly, she said:

"There's really nothing much I can say about myself except that I was born and raised in this city. I did all my schooling here, and today, as an Accountant, I'm employed in a great Bank. I'm an only child, and I think, generally, God has been exceedingly kind to me, especially for giving me the kind of family that I have. My parents are fantastic; to have brought me up with the utmost regard for God, the way they had done, I can't thank them enough for that, and I couldn't have asked for more from God. Given the option, I shall choose my mom and dad a million times over."

Obinna listened intently but did not really know how to respond. Here was somebody who was so proud of her parents, but could he say the same thing about his own parents? No, he was not sure he could. He was from, more or less, a dysfunctional family where his parents got regularly into frequent brawls over money issues. He was the second of five boys in a troubled, poverty-stricken home where the parents eventually separated because of seemingly unending money quarrels. Growing up had been tough, even in the university where he had to support himself partly from the paltry sum he got from his father, and partly through organising summer classes for secondary school students. When he remained silent and did not say anything, Martha gently asked him to tell her about himself. This brought him back to reality from his brief reverie. Perhaps he did not expect that question because, instantly, his facial muscles started twitching slowly as was always the case with him. Martha saw the twitching muscles, focused her attention on it, but the twitches rapidly became worse as she gazed at him. Suspecting she was the cause of the sudden worsening twitching; she slowly turned her head, and looked away.

"Does that happen to you always, or are you nervous because of me?" Martha asked him very nicely, attempting to put him at his ease, when the twitches abated.

"No, I'm not nervous because of you, Martha," he responded and managed to force a laugh as though he hadn't heard of anything more ridiculous. "It's something that happens to me from time to time," he told her somewhat bashfully, "Please, think nothing of it."

"There could be a medical reason for it," Martha said to him gently, "Have you tried consulting your doctor about it?"

"Please, Martha. It is not a medical condition. It is something that I have had since childhood. Please, take no further thought to it."

Martha said nothing further, but she tried not to look directly at him, afraid she might trigger another series of facial twitches in him.

This was followed by a prolonged silence.

"Look, Martha," he said suddenly; breaking the silence, "I'm going to cut the chase with you and go straight to the point. I asked you here for a reason, the reason being that I think I'm going crazy because of you. I'm madly in love with you, Martha. Since that day I met you in Babatunde's house, I have not been able to get you out of my head."

Martha laughed softly in her uniquely charming manner. She seemed very amused. In her opinion, Obinna, though very matured, was behaving like a teenage secondary school boy.

"Mr. Obinna," she addressed him by name still with the radiant smile on her face, "Couldn't you have waited for us to get better acquainted before telling me what you just told me?" Without waiting for a reply, she said, "I think it is better to say such things to people we know reasonably well. Anyway, I hope you don't expect a reply from me now because I can't give you any yet. Moreover, I know virtually nothing about you."

A worried look instantly crept onto Obinna's face.

"Why, Martha?" He queried. "Don't you like me?"

"Looking the way you do, Mr. Obinna," she responded with gaiety, "You are a big catch for any girl. But relationships must not be based entirely on mere physical appearance. Compatibility of the persons involved in a romantic relationship is of the essence. Please, tell me about yourself, Mr. Obinna."

This was the moment that Obinna dreaded the most because it was certain to bring out their differences which had long been a cause of much concern and worry for him.

"Well," he began, trying to sound confident, "I was born and raised in this city just like you; but unlike you, I have four brothers, and I'm the second born of my parents. All my schooling was also done in this city, and I graduated in Philosophy from the University a couple of years ago. Currently, I'm engaged in a business deal with Babatunde. That was the reason you saw me in his house the other day."

A look of concern suddenly appeared in Martha's eyes at the mention of Babatunde's name. She had her reservations about Babatunde; something had instinctively warned her against him the first time she met him. If not for the sake of her friend, Juliette, who literally forced her to his house on the three occasions she had been there, left to her own options, she would not go within a mile of Babatunde's house. Moreover, after the event in that house the last time she visited; when Juliette had scolded her like a child, just because she indicated her interest to attend Church, she had resolved never to set foot again in the house.

"What is the problem?" Obinna asked her, "You seemed a little worried when I mentioned Babatunde's name."

There was a pause before Martha answered.

"I just want to let you know that you should be very careful of Babatunde," she said to him very slowly and emphatically, "A good name is better than riches. Sadly, Babatunde does not have a good reputation."

"I can hardly see why," interjected Obinna. "Babatunde is one of the most truthful and kindest persons I've ever met."

There was a pause again before Martha responded.

"So he seemed on the surface," she told him very emphatically again. "But be careful in whatever business dealings you have with him. There might be some elements of truth in the rumours that have been circulated about him in public."

"I don't listen to cheap gossip," responded Obinna, "They were spread by people who envied his overwhelming success, and could never hope to compete successfully with him in anything."

Martha said nothing further about Babatunde.

"At least I have warned him," she said to herself, "It is left to him either to take, or refuse, my advice."

All of a sudden, Martha changed the subject, and said:

"I'm a Christian, Mr. Obinna, of the Catholic Faith, and I attend Mass regularly at St. Christopher's Cathedral in Lagos Island. What about you, Mr. Obinna? I suspect you are also a Christian, but of which denomination, and which Church do you worship?"

Obinna felt as though iced, cold water had been thrown suddenly in his face, and almost immediately, his facial muscles started firing away, very haphazardly, to his utmost embarrassment. Martha instinctively looked away from him, feeling sorry that, perhaps, her steady gaze at him had triggered those twitches again. However, after a few minutes, by a great effort of the Will, he forced himself to relax, and the twitches eventually subsided.

"I'm really sorry, Mr. Obinna, if I'm the one making you this nervous," Martha said to him in a very sympathetic voice. "But I want you to know that not for all the world will I ever upset or embarrass you in anyway about anything. I'm sincerely pleading with you, Mr. Obinna, to please, relax in my company now and always. There's absolutely nothing to fear in me."

"I should be the one apologising to you, Martha," he told her in a low bashful voice after a short pause. "My face twitch sporadically from time to time as I explained earlier to you. I was born with it, and had to live with it. To get back to your question, Martha. I'm a Freethinker, and don't attend any church and I…"

"Just a moment, Mr. Obinna," Martha said in a moderately loud voice, deeply astounded, and cutting him short at mid-sentence. "When you described yourself as a Freethinker, what do you mean precisely? Do you believe in Jesus Christ and in God for instance?"

This was the moment of truth for Obinna as he was being confronted directly with what he feared the most. Should he tell this very attractive, young, female specimen whom he wanted so much, a lie, as this would increase his chances of winning her, or should he tell her the truth and damn the consequences as he had told himself that he would always do in matters of religion: which is never to hide the truth about his beliefs? He sat there with her, his head slightly bent, his eyes carefully avoiding hers, and looking directly at the table, trying desperately to reach an answer to her question; while she, sitting directly opposite him, held herself fully erect with her eyes fixed on his massive head waiting for his response.

After the prolonged and awkward hesitation, Obinna suddenly looked up directly into her deeply inquiring eyes:

"I will not lie to you, or deceive you, Martha," he said to her. "I'll tell you the absolute truth about my convictions... I don't believe in Christianity, I don't believe in any God, and I certainly don't believe in Jesus Christ."

Now it was Martha who felt as though iced, cold water had been thrown so recklessly in her face. Absolutely shocked beyond description, she just sat there scarcely believing what she had just heard, more so, from a man who had just sought her friendship. In all her twenty-eight years of existence, this was the first time she was meeting, and as a matter of fact, sitting with someone who completely denied the existence of the Almighty God and of His Christ, both of whom were so dear to her, and had been brought up to revere with absolute devotion, trust and faith, and to believe in, unflinchingly, all through her life, even to the death.

When she recovered a little from her immense shock; her first thought was to get up, pick up her bag, and walk away; and never have anything again to do with this enigmatic being known as Obinna Kelechi. However, on second thought, she decided against it. She remained seated in her chair but did not say anything for a long time. The two of them just sat there together, in the awkward silence, musing.

"So, you don't believe in God, Mr. Obinna," she addressed him eventually, somewhat coldly, and the friendly smile had disappeared completely from her face. "You don't believe in

God, and you dare to hint, or even suggest, at the possibility of a relationship between us?"

Obinna Kelechi did not say anything.

"Let me tell you outrightly now," she continued, her eyes flashing, "Let me give my reply to you now, Mr. Obinna, so that you don't waste your time any further in regard to what you said earlier about your inability to get me out of your head. My reply to you is that such a relationship can never exist between us. Not because I don't like you as a man, for if I don't, I wouldn't even show up here in the first instance, but because such a relationship will never work between us for the reason that our differences shall be completely irreconcilable as I can never compromise my Christian Faith for anything else in this world."

Obinna did not say anything, he merely watched her, avoided her eyes as much as he could, for he seemed a little afraid of her now. A sort of mysterious light was beginning to shine in her eyes as she spoke.

"I will ask you this question," she continued, "Mr. Obinna, did you create yourself?"

Obinna did not respond.

"Lift up your eyes," she said, "Lift them up far beyond this earth, and consider the tremendous forces of nature. Consider the solar system, the earth and the planets—spinning at astonishing speed around the giant sun—yet their very motions are so coordinated, so regulated, that the position of any planet can be determined at any point in time with mathematical exactitude far in advance. What do you call that, Mr. Obinna? Order, or Disorder? Which of the two is a more natural state?"

Obinna still did not say anything. He just kept mute.

"Does Science not teach us that Disorder is a more natural state?" Martha said to him, "And that a force is always needed to maintain order in any system. Leave your kitchen, your garden, or your living room unattended for just a few days, and you'll marvel at the disorderly state and mess you'll find it. If such a thing as trifling as keeping your home neat requires a force or effort to maintain it in a state of order, how much more the gigantic forces that maintain the profound order we perceive out there in the Cosmos; and you tell me there is no God?"

He shifted uneasily in his chair but said nothing.

"Come out of your apartment at midnight," she told him, "Come out on a clear, dark, moonless night; stand in your balcony; look up at the sky, and you might see the Constellation of Orion, or even the spiral Galaxy of Andromeda, and tell me if such awesome beauties just existed on their own without a Maker. What keeps all the planets, all the stars and the hundreds of billions of galaxies in their perpetual state of ordered uniform motion?" Martha asked him with an expectant look in her eyes.

Still, Obinna did not attempt to answer. He either does not know the answer, or he was just being reticent.

"Divine Power does the work," she told him the answer, "And another name for it is the 'Word of God!' The Spiritual force that nourishes and sustains this universe; that also maintains that perfect order never fails, Mr. Obinna. Oh, no, it never fails! Have you ever thought, have you ever imagined, what could possibly happen were the force to fail for just a fraction of a second, and the earth, for instance, veered off its divinely assigned orbit? The result would be absolutely catastrophic, and all life would be extinguished on the earth in an instant! But the 'Word of God,' the divine Love of the Everlasting Father, would never allow such a tragic occurrence. From everlasting to everlasting, the Word of God, also known as Jesus Christ, maintains this absolute Peace and never-failing Order in the Universe. Perhaps that is why He is also known as the 'Prince of Peace!'"

Obinna shifted again in his chair. He still could not venture a word in defence of his own philosophy. He merely continued to watch

Martha in deep fascination for she looked wonderfully beautiful as she spoke—like an Angel; and the light that flashed in her eyes simply amazed him. Never had he seen any woman speak with such authority and ardour.

"That Word of God was made flesh," Martha resumed, "And He came down into this world, being born of a Virgin. He came that He might show us the way to everlasting life. He was crucified and died as was ordained by the Father, but resurrected from the dead on the third day, and ascended back into heaven from whence He came. Through the shedding of His divine blood, He ransomed all of lost humanity back unto the Father—all of humanity, Mr. Obinna—and that includes you, me, and everyone else."

There was a slight pause here, and both of them exchanged glances.

"Dear, Mr. Obinna." Martha implored him gently, "Please, for your own sake, embrace Christ Jesus our Saviour. Come with me to

Church, and let us go through these things that I've been discussing with you in greater details."

Then she extended her hand to him as she invited him to Church, her symbol of acceptance and friendship. However, Obinna Kelechi, adamant as ever, did not respond. He did not take her hand. He just sat there looking at the hand; for taking that hand would symbolize the abandonment of his own philosophy and his acquiescence—his acceptance of Christianity. He was not ready to abandon his philosophy, a philosophy that he had nurtured and espoused for much of his adult life.

When he did not take the hand she had offered him, Martha gently withdrew her hand. They sat there together in that strained silence with no further words exchanged between them. Then suddenly, the wall clock in the restaurant chimed the hour of 9:00 pm, thus breaking the uneasy silence. Martha stood up instantly, told him quietly that she had overstayed, and would like to leave.

He stood up too.

"Please, Mr. Obinna," Martha addressed him as soon as he got to his feet, "I want you to keep thinking about the things we have discussed here, tonight, and I know that God will certainly give you a true knowledge of Himself one day. Meanwhile, I'll always remember and mention you in my prayers."

He did not respond as he does not believe in any form of prayer to any deity. They both walked to the exit of the restaurant after he had settled all the bills.

"How did you get here?" He asked her—at last breaking his long silence—as they walked to the parking lot.

"I came in my car," Martha answered, "What about you?"

"A driver will soon be here to pick me up."

"Instead of waiting here alone, I can drop you off at your place. It will be my pleasure, please, Mr. Obinna."

"Do not bother," he responded. "The driver just sent me a text message that he is almost here."

"Alright," Martha said.

Then she thanked him sincerely for the time spent together, entered her *Hyundai Elantra*, and drove off while he stood waving at her till the car disappeared from his sight.

Chapter 11

Several weeks later, Martha and Juliette were seated opposite each another in the restaurant of the Acme City Bank where Martha was employed. Juliette, also an Accountant, was well supplied with good cash on a regular basis by Babatunde, and thought it unnecessary to work. Thus, she spends most of her time just looking beautiful for Babatunde. She had paid an unexpected visit to Martha in the Bank, and both ladies had embraced and greeted each other so heartily. Since the little incident in Babatunde's house several months ago, these two ladies had neither seen nor communicated much with each other, except by very occasional phone calls. They were sharing their experiences together in the last few months over a few bottles of soft drinks at the restaurant. Martha was dressed in a gorgeous, black suit. A beautiful white bead adorned her neck. Her soft smooth skin was radiant as ever; and her face—fresh without freckles—glowed in the light. She looked as lovely and elegant as ever. Juliette was in tight-fitting jeans trousers and T-shirt with a baseball cap on her head. Her long shiny hair flowed freely on her shoulders, and she looked very beautiful.

"Babatunde and I are getting married very soon," said Juliette excitedly, "We have set the date for the 30th of October, roughly six months from now, I hope you'll be there, Martha?"

"Certainly," replied Martha, "I won't miss your wedding for anything in the world, and I'm very happy for you, Juliette."

"That is the problem," Juliette said with a frown, "You are happy for me, but I can't say the same thing exactly about you."

"Why?" Martha asked, looking a little concerned.

"Look girl, I'm really worried about you," began Juliette, "You need a man in your life. Since our university days, when I first met you, you've never really had a boyfriend, or gone steady with any man."

A faint smile lit up Martha's face but she did not say anything.

"I can remember," Juliette continued, "I can remember that I've introduced several guys to you: Emeka, Segun, Michael and many others. Guys that are very rich and good looking—the crème de la crème of society—and the most eligible bachelors in this town. But after one or two outings with them, you usually call off the relationship. Why, Martha, why? Don't you ever want to settle down and get married like everyone else? We are both twenty-eight years old now, and in a few months' time, you will be twenty-nine; two months before I turn twenty-nine too. We're not really so young again, Martha. Don't be fooled by your youthful looks and great beauty now because once a woman turns thirty; her beauty begins to fade slowly, and then rapidly when she turns thirty-five."

Martha laughed loudly, seeming very amused at her friend's mistaken beliefs about the beauty of a woman, for Martha knew with certainty that some women remained beautiful well past the age of eighty years, and some, all through their lives.

"Look, Martha," continued Juliette, "I can understand your devotion to Christianity—and please, I do apologize for the way I spoke to you the last time we were together in Babatunde's house—but it is my candid opinion that you are overdoing this religious stuff. I don't think you should allow it to hinder you from living your life fully. You need to find a man, Martha, to love and settle down with."

"Thank you very much," Martha responded with a smile, "Thank you for your great concern about me, Juliette. But I must plead very sincerely with you to stop worrying about me because I am quite at peace with the world. The peace and joy which I enjoy, I'll not lose for all the world; certainly not if I can help it because I'm aware they are the gifts of God to me. I know that in our society, one can hardly be considered happy or successful in any endeavour if one is not married, no matter how well or how great that person's achievements were. However, Juliette, I'll tell you very honestly that I'd rather remain single all my life than exchange place with any of the seemingly happily married women in our society. Many women—and I know a great deal of them—do not enjoy their marriages but simply endure them. These women lacked peace of mind; they feel totally frustrated, unhappy and disillusioned with what was meant to be a holy wedlock. I know this fact, Juliette, because many of them have confided their frustrations in me. And as for the guys you introduced to me, I thank you once again for your concern and kind gesture. But none of them understood what love really meant let alone how to express it. They were simply lusting after me, and wanted to possess me as though I'm a property of sorts, to be purchased, and possessed as one might possess a house or a car. Juliette, you would have been so amazed if you had seen their eagerness in showing me how wealthy they were. They consistently dangled money in my face, just like an angler dangles a worm at the end of his fishing line, and expected me to swallow it all—hook, line and sinker—like an unfortunate fish would swallow the worm on the fishing line. They never seemed to stop talking of their achievements, their properties and everything they owned. Unfortunately for the poor Souls, I'm not the type of woman anyone can influence, or tempt with such things."

There was a slight pause here before Martha continued.

"I do not lack love, Juliette, as you inferred earlier. As a matter of fact, I'm overwhelmed by it. The young orphans that I've taken charge of lavish me abundantly with it; the great women with whom I…"

"I know, I know," interjected Juliette, "I know you are involved in a lot of charitable works, and that you are such a great blessing in the lives of many people. I also know that all the activities make you really glow with warmth, very happily inside. But what I'm talking about, Martha, is a man's love. Not the type your little orphans show you, my dear friend. I'm talking about a real man's love: to be embraced by a man, to be cuddled by a man, and to be kissed passionately by a man—that is what I'm talking about, Martha."

Martha smiled softly as her eyes suddenly flashed.

"A man's love," she said firmly, "A real man's love, and what is that, Juliette? What is it worth? If you understand the true nature of an average man, well enough, Juliette, you would not talk the way you just did."

Juliette leaned forward in her chair, eager to hear more of what she scornfully termed a 'Sermon on love' in her heart.

"A man may profess to love you," Martha continued, "He may profess to love you more than anything else in the world this very minute, but the moment you turn your head, he is declaring the same love to another woman, even to your best friend, or your blood sister! That is not love, dearest Juliette, but a sham of it. It is mere animalism, the primeval desire of the male to mate with the female. We perceive it amongst animals, and also amongst humankind. It is completely different from love. Nothing is more fickle than the love of a man. It lacks the element of trust, and so, it isn't worth very much. Any woman who relied on such a love would soon be brought to a very rude awakening. Isn't that the reason why divorce rates are so outrageously high in virtually all societies of the world today, Juliette?"

Juliette smiled mockingly, but nodded her head in agreement.

"A man's love does not pass the test of time," Martha continued, "It waxes cold with time, withers like a dying flower, and then like smoke, it totally disappears. I wouldn't trade the love of my little orphans, as you called them,

Juliette, for the sham form of it that exists in the world today."

There was a long pause as Juliette was a little astonished at her friend's candour on the issue of Love. She thought Martha's view, or opinion on love was weird.

"But do you ever dream of love?" Juliette asked her, after the pause, with a surprised note in her voice.

"O yes, I do sometimes, especially in my sleep when I'm dreaming," Martha responded. "Not the sham form of it, but the real Love, the one that lasts forever—Love Everlasting. The love that I dream of can hardly be found in this world, Juliette, which is why I'm not in a hurry. I know I'll realize that Love someday," she said somewhat rapturously. "I know I'll realize that Love without fail, Juliette, even if it is after I've departed this world... anytime the Author and Creator of my Soul decree it."

"What more can I say?" Juliette suddenly said with a sigh. Then she stood up slowly, shrugged her shoulders, as though she was giving up on Martha, and she seemed ready to take her leave.

Martha got up too, and they both walked in silence towards Juliette's massive SUV in the parking lot.

"Are you getting on well with Mr. Obinna?" Juliette suddenly asked as they walked together. "I was the one who gave your phone number to him when he asked Babatunde for it. Sorry I didn't ask your permission before I did that."

"No, Juliette, you need not apologise," Martha responded, "That is not a problem. But how I fared with him is a discussion for another day, Juliette." Martha said with a sigh. "A gist for another day, Juliette. I promise you, we'll discuss it later because my lunch break is almost over, and I have to get back to my office in a hurry before my absence is noticed in the Bank."

When they reached the parking lot, Juliette climbed into the SUV, and started the engine while Martha waved at her.

Suddenly the window of the SUV opened, and Juliette stuck her head out of it.

"Can you, please, visit me tomorrow?" She asked Martha somewhat timidly, "In my fiancé, Babatunde's house in the evening after you clock out of work?"

Martha, a little taken by surprise, quickly composed herself. She remembered she had an engagement tomorrow in the evening.

"Please, Juliette," she told her, "You have to excuse me as I intend to attend Mass at the Convent with Abbess Morenike Oluwaseun after work tomorrow."

Juliette smiled, a derisive smile, but said nothing. However, in her heart, her thoughts essentially were, "Waste your life away because of religion if you like. Heaven knows that I've done my part, as a good friend, and warned you. We shall soon find out where all these excessive devotion to Christianity will lead you."

The window of the SUV closed. Then Juliette reversed, and sent the SUV flying recklessly into the road while Martha stood there, still waving at Juliette, with a smile on her face, till the SUV turned out of her sight.

CHAPTER 12

Few months later, Monica and Obinna were seen shopping together in the various shops of the ever-busy Balogun street in Lagos. Monica, holding Obinna by the hand, walked him excitedly from shop to shop, examining various articles, and picking up one item here, one there, talking and laughing loudly as they went. They walked happily from boutique to boutique, and were even the envy of some passers-by who turned their heads repeatedly to admire them. Relationship had improved tremendously between them. Obinna, after his outright failure with Martha that evening at the restaurant of King-sized Delights, had found some solace in the arms of

Monica who was anxiously waiting for him at home that evening. He had told her a lie about being involved in a late-business meeting when he got home. Monica, having succeeded in forcing her way back into his life that night she returned, had remained with him since. They were once again living together as they did some years ago before she walked out on him so unceremoniously. Later, Monica had contacted her sixty-two year old fiancé, informed him as nicely as she could, that she was no longer interested in him, and returned his ring to him. The man was instantly broken-hearted, and almost in tears as he took the ring from her reluctantly. He tried to ask how he had wronged her. But, before he could say anything, Monica had disappeared. She seemed to have an unpleasant knack of walking out so abruptly on the men she was romantically involved with.

However, there was a problem. Obinna was still hopelessly and helplessly obsessed with Martha. The events of that night at King-sized Delights still haunt him. Martha looked more beautiful and more charming than any woman he had ever set his eyes upon. He thought she looked like one of those enchantingly-beautiful Greek goddesses whose statues still adorn some preserved, historical sites of ancient Greece. He had seen the pictures of many of such statues in some of his precious books, and had always been enthralled at their ravishing beauty. And the way Martha spoke so ardently and so confidently about her beliefs deeply impressed him. He felt sorry for himself, knowing he was already flowing smoothly with her during their conversation that evening, and he knew he was inches away from winning her, had the issue of religion not come to fore.

"Cursed religion!" He said to himself, "Always causing divisions and wars."

Notwithstanding what happened that night, he remained hopeful and told himself he would give her another call later, and invite her out again. He had since made up his mind to tell her a lie about his readiness to accept Christianity. This was just a trick to get her attention, bring her closer, and eventually make her his; as he was not in the least interested in Christianity—for he hated Christianity in its totality.

"But what about Monica?" He had asked himself this question severally.

Though he liked Monica better now than when she came back newly into his life; love, however, was out of the question. He assured himself that he had warned her, that same night she returned, that he no longer loved her, and would not be responsible for anything that happened to her. Monica, as far as he was concerned, would constitute herself a barrier in his bid to win Martha's affections. Martha, for instance, if ever she became a close friend of his, would never agree to visit him at home with Monica under the same roof. In fact, the outcome of such an occurrence was unthinkable. He realized the issue was now far more complicated than he had imagined.

"This is now what they call, 'A love triangle,'" he told himself, "Two is company, and three is a crowd. There's bound to be complications. We shall see how things pan out."

"Let's leave now, sweetheart," said Monica suddenly, interrupting his thoughts, and forcing them back to the present. Her high-pitched voice rang out in loud and clear accents, "We are done with shopping for now."

Obinna stooped instinctively, and picked up two of the three large package of goods and groceries while Monica picked up the third one, and they both walked towards the parking lot. Babatunde had presented Obinna with the keys of a brand new *Mercedes Benz C Class Saloon Car,* two weeks earlier. This was followed by a gift of another bulky brown envelope containing exactly one million naira, handed over to Obinna directly by Babatunde. The money, according to Babatunde, was meant to fuel Obinna's new car. That was merely figurative as the money was really meant for Obinna's upkeep. One million naira just for fuelling was a monumental exaggeration. Obinna, deeply astounded, had thanked Babatunde so effusively till he became absolutely speechless. Thereafter, Babatunde had assigned one of his chauffeurs to Obinna. He taught Obinna how to drive confidently in three days. Obinna could drive the car virtually anywhere in Lagos now. He got into the driver's seat, and Monica sat proudly beside him at the passenger side. He started the engine, and then screeched the car loudly into the road.

Many months passed quickly without any event. It was on a Friday morning when Obinna and Monica were having breakfast together that Babatunde called him quite unexpectedly on his cell phone.

"I'll like to see you right away in my house." Babatunde told him succinctly on the telephone.

"No problem," Obinna responded, "I'll be with you shortly."

Both men hung up.

"That was my business partner," Obinna told Monica at the dining table. "He wants me to come around to his place right away to consider a very important business proposal together."

"When can I meet him?" Monica asked, "Can I go with you now?"

"No, not today, sweetheart," he responded. "We have work to do now. Don't worry, honey. We'll visit him together someday in the evening when he isn't very busy."

With that said, Obinna gobbled down his breakfast, and said goodbye to Monica with a kiss. Minutes later, he was driving as fast as he could to Babatunde's house.

He got to Babatunde's house, and met what seemed like a full house there. There were ten men including Babatunde in one of the large living rooms in the house. They were men from various professional backgrounds and nationals. Four of them, including Babatunde, were from the country; but the rest of them were expatriates from North Africa, Europe, and Asia. They were all very fine and highly successful looking men. They were cultured in their manners, and exhibited a lot of suavity. Their ages range from thirty-five to seventy years. They had gathered in Babatunde's house, at his request, for a little get-together. Obinna was immediately introduced by Babatunde to each of the men who shook hands vigorously with him in a very friendly manner. These men were the heads of various organizations—Chief Executives, Managing Directors, Politicians and Chairmen of highly successful world-class organizations spread across the globe.

"Welcome, Mr. Obinna Kelechi." They all said to him gaily.

"Thank you, sirs." Obinna responded to them. But to him, the greeting was rather strange, "Welcome to where or what?" He wondered uneasily.

"Please, Obinna. Kindly join us for lunch," Babatunde announced. "We were waiting for you to join us before we start."

Though he had just had breakfast with Monica, Obinna did not object. He still had enough room in his stomach to accommodate more food. They all proceeded to the dining room where varieties of excellent meals had been prepared by Babatunde's chefs, and were served by the numerous servants in attendance. The best wines were served, and their conversations at the table were mainly of a general nature: business, politics, the stock market, who is making the biggest money and how. After lunch, the guests started departing one after the other, shaking hands, and thanking Babatunde for hosting them generously. This continued until only Obinna and Babatunde remained in the house.

"Those men," began Babatunde in a casual manner, "Are fellow members of the society that I belong—*the Great Lucide'il Society.* It is one of the most exclusive societies under the sun, and members enjoy untold privileges amongst which are: great wealth beyond anyone's imagination, power and influence over virtually all circumstances in every government and country on this planet, free admittance into the most exclusive places or clubs in any country. Those men exercise enormous control over the governments of their various countries, and largely determine the economic fortunes of the world. It is very difficult to accept new members into the Society, and any potential new member is usually taken through series of very rigorous screening processes, and even at that, most applicants are rejected. However, before your arrival here today, Obinna, I discussed you extensively with them, and suggested you as a potential member. I gave them a brief history of your background, résumé, and circumstance. All the members were very pleased and agreed to have you join the Society as soon as you wish. That was only possible because I, as the current Chairman of the Society, recommended you."

Babatunde's words sounded like music to Obinna's ears. He felt instantly elated, highly pleased, to be considered for the membership of a society that exercised sway over the world's wealth and economy. This certainly was a rare privilege for him. That was exactly what he had always wished for virtually all his life.

THE PACT

"Thank you, Babatunde." He responded heartily, "I'll be more than grateful to you if you can enlist me as a member of the Society."

"So, are you giving me your consent to enrol you as a member of the *Great Lucide'il* Society?" Babatunde asked him with a sudden seriousness in his voice.

"Absolutely," came the reply.

"Okay," said Babatunde, "I'll facilitate the process and get you enlisted as soon as possible. I'll also ensure that you're exempted from all routine screening processes."

"Wow!" Obinna screamed. Then he jumped up very excitedly, clapped his hands, and said, "Thank you very much, Babatunde. I shall never forget this for the rest of my life!"

"Now, Obinna," Babatunde said somewhat gravely, "To address the question you've been pestering me with for many months now, I mean your constant queries about the source of my wealth. I believe the time has come for me to divulge that secret to you since you are so hell-bent on knowing the truth about my wealth."

"At last!" Obinna screamed happily again, "So, you now count me worthy to be let into your secret of wealth, Babatunde. Words can't describe the depth of my gratitude to you. I shall remain grateful to you for as long as I live, Babatunde. You're the truest and best friend I've ever had, and a brother indeed."

But Babatunde did not respond. He was silent for a while, looked up suddenly, but still did not say anything. Then he brought his face gradually downwards, and met Obinna's eyes fixedly. After a few seconds of sustained eye-to-eye contact between them, Babatunde, somewhat grimly, said:

"I'm one of the chief recruiters for Lucifer!"

Chapter 13

Obinna suddenly let out a wild discordant laughter, his laughter—very loud and harsh—seemed to be echoed by the very roof and walls of the entire house while Babatunde watched and scoffed intensely at him. When he was done with laughing, he looked at Babatunde, saw the deep scorn in his eyes, but was undaunted.

"Joshua Anjorin Babatunde," he addressed him by his full name, "I know you've always been a mysterious fellow. That is very clear from the wild way you talk most times, and the way you conduct yourself, but little did I suspect that you are also going slowly over the edge!"

Babatunde did not answer. He merely watched Obinna with deepening interest and contempt.

"Who, or what, had deceived you into believing such hogwash?" Obinna asked him, "Apparently, you've learned nothing from all I've been discussing with you for many months now. There is no such thing or personage as Lucifer, or the devil. Please, my friend, wake up from the deep slumber of ignorance you've fallen pitifully into. I thought you a wise man with sense, Babatunde. But what a disappointment you turned out to be!"

Obinna went on and on with statements like these without Babatunde bothering to respond. Eventually he stopped, speechless, and a little breathless.

"Are you done ridiculing and insulting me, Obinna?" Babatunde asked him, "Are you quite done now? Every fool must learn the hard way, and I don't think I have ever met a bigger one than you, Obinna! Now, listen attentively to what I'm about to relate to you, for your own sake, Obinna, as your future depends largely on it."

Obinna, very surprised at how Babatunde was speaking, listened.

"My wealth," began Babatunde in a very solemn voice, "My vast and seemingly inexhaustible wealth that you have coveted in your dark and selfish heart all the while was given to me by the devil—every little bit of it!"

Obinna looked at him, he seemed the same Babatunde he had always known, but that composure and calm that always characterized him appeared to have waned, for he seemed a little frazzled now. What strange malady had afflicted Babatunde, and was causing him to rant at something not true, something not real, and something not in existence? Obinna wondered.

"Several years ago," Babatunde said, "I was a homeless waif and penniless like you were, Obinna. I was on the verge of committing suicide, being in very deep and unremitting anguish until I met Lucifer. I was recruited for him by one of his followers who knew that I was about to kill myself. It was a direct bargain with the devil—my Soul for the riches—that was all. Lucifer bought my Soul; and the riches which you have also partaken of, and coveted secretly, is the price of my Soul!"

"O there he goes again," Obinna mused, "Now he is talking about a Soul, another non-existent thing, an absolute nonentity. How and when did this guy sink to this level of insanity?"

"I know you think me mad, Obinna." Babatunde said, "I can read it in your thoughts and in your heart, but it doesn't change the facts. Everyone who has come under the influence and control of Satan is charged with the responsibility of bringing Souls to him. The kingdom of darkness is forever at work, never resting for a single moment. I have already recruited two Souls for him, Obinna, you were intended to be my third and final candidate! However, this is possible only if you wish, only if you agree, or desire to join! There is no use of force, people are recruited entirely on their own freewill; entirely on their own volition to join Lucifer, and are never forced. They may be enticed, or tempted, but never forced."

Babatunde paused for a few moments here during which he glared at Obinna, expecting to hear his comments. However, Obinna did not say anything.

"If you join him," Babatunde resumed, "Lucifer takes your Soul, and in return, he rewards you with wealth far beyond your capacity to use and enjoy. When we, the followers of Lucifer, seek out our victims, it is always the downtrodden, those at the throes of starvation, or death, who need desperate help in society that we target, for such are the ones who will quickly fall prey to us. People that are well-to-do, or who have reasonable sources of income, or wealth, like gainfully employed individuals, or professionals, don't readily agree to join us, and are not always our prime targets."

Obinna stood looking at Babatunde, listening to what he was saying in utter amazement, that Obinna felt so irritated at what he termed, "The vituperations of a madman," in his heart.

"You were targeted right from the outset, Obinna, because of the dire circumstances you lived in. I manipulated you psychically right from the beginning of our association together, or friendship, if I can call it that! The interview you attended at the Bureau House was a hoax, set up by me and my agents. Likewise all other job interviews you attended within the last five years. Those interviews were set up by me and my agents to frustrate you with failures after failures in order to drive you to the edge of insanity, and make you far more vulnerable for easy manipulation by the forces of darkness. I followed you after the interview at the Bureau House, watched you, and when you suddenly fainted in the streets from lack of food, it was as if fate itself was on my side, and against you, for it gave me the exact opportunity I needed to dominate you completely and make you absolutely dependent upon me."

THE PACT

There was an eerie silence here as Babatunde paused again for a few moments. Obinna could hardly believe his ears, all interviews he had attended within the last five years were set up and manipulated by Babatunde? Could he believe that? But the first time he ever saw him was at the hospital, less than two years ago, how could Babatunde have evaded him all these while?

"And from the way things have gone between us, Obinna," Babatunde resumed suddenly, "Since that first time at St. Mary's Hospital till now, you can see that I have largely succeeded with you. If you come to Lucifer, Obinna, he dusts and cleans you up completely and transforms you into an international figure, highly successful. All the fine looking and very successful gentlemen you met here earlier today, all of whom are controlling world-class super businesses and the world governments, were once people who were completely broke, downtrodden, and many of them had lived on food picked from dustbins!"

"Enough of this wild talk, Babatunde!" Obinna suddenly shouted at him, "You need psychiatric help desperately, and I'll find a Psychiatrist for you!"

"Insult me all you like, Obinna," interrupted Babatunde, "But I've laid it all wide-open to you. The ball is in your very court now. All you need to do is to make a decision, just one huge decision that will determine your future from now henceforth. Choose Lucifer, and you will be one of the richest men in the world, adored and praised by all; you will have your pick of the choicest women anywhere in the world, as many you wish. Governments will carry out all your biddings without questions, you will have the world at your feet. But reject Lucifer, and you're back on the streets and into that rat hole where you crawled out of. Your girlfriend will run away again like she did the last time when you were completely broke, and could not even afford to give her a decent meal, or buy her nice clothing."

"How did this raving madman know about Monica?" Obinna wondered as he was sure he had not said anything about Monica to him yet.

"Failure to make a choice," Babatunde continued, "Is regarded as a rejection by Lucifer, and so, all the conditions of rejection applies: direst poverty, squalor, loss of integrity and self-respect, as well as loss of all the gains you think you've already made with the devil's money. And don't deceive yourself, my friend, by thinking that you've already invested part of the money that I've been giving to you in profitable ventures; because immediately you reject Lucifer, or fail to make a decision now, all those investments will crumble and go to huge waste, for they are investments wrought with the devil's money. That is the way Lucifer operates, he doesn't give anything free to anybody."

Obinna continued to stare at Babatunde in disbelief. Babatunde was not only talking wildly but his eyes were also wild, and had taken on a red hue. He seemed entirely schizophrenic to Obinna at this point. Surely, Babatunde would benefit from Psychiatric help now; he would find a Psychiatrist for him once he left the house Obinna told himself again.

"You must make your choice now, Obinna, because time is very short." Babatunde interrupted Obinna's thoughts again, "You must make that choice now," he stated emphatically again.

"Alright, alright!" Obinna yelled, out of sheer frustration, "Babatunde," he said, "You have spoken at great lengths, but I don't believe any of what you've been ranting about since. I am certain that there is nothing like Lucifer, or the devil, in existence as you have suggested all along like a madman that I'm convinced you are now. Therefore, if it makes you feel any better, I'll tell you my choice right away!"

Obinna paused at this point while all of Babatunde's nerves were stretched almost to breaking point, watching Obinna anxiously, and waiting eagerly to hear his choice.

"I choose Lucifer," Obinna said, "I choose the devil!"

THE PACT

An absolute and uneasy silence instantly followed the unholy choice made by Obinna as though the very elements themselves were struck speechless by the sheer horror of such a choice.

"Thank you, Obinna," Babatunde said in earnest, breaking the silence with a huge sigh of relief. "Your choice of Lucifer frees me and fulfils my obligations to him. I couldn't have been able to harm you, Obinna, or do anything to you had you rejected him. It only means that I must look for another candidate before my time runs out. Thank you once again," Babatunde repeated, feeling somewhat relieved and grateful. "I'll alert members of the Society that you've agreed to join, and we shall perform the initiation as soon as possible without any waste of time."

Obinna scoffed at Babatunde very intensely.

"Lunatic!" He called Babatunde in a loud voice.

Without another word, Obinna prepared to take his leave. He turned and headed straight for the door.

"I'll inform you!" Babatunde cried, as Obinna opened the door, "I'll inform you as soon as the Society chooses the date for your initiation—your initiation into the family of the devil!" Then he roared with a loud derisive laughter as Obinna stepped outside and slammed the door shut.

Chapter 14

Three weeks later, in a large dimly-lit and carefully-concealed hall on the top floor of Joshua Anjorin Babatunde's magnificent house, were ten persons; all apparelled in dark, flowing hoods. They had gathered there for a secret purpose, and Babatunde, with a profound air of authority, was in their midst. His head was slightly exposed, and his face, though still handsome, was dark, and exhibited a subtle grave aspect. On it was that ever-present whimsical smile. All the ten hooded figures surrounded Obinna who was ordinarily dressed, and seated on a low stool in their midst. On his face was a scornful look, for up till this moment, he still maintained that Babatunde had been talking wildly, and probably suffered from some strange malady of the mind. He had not believed all what Babatunde had been telling him in the past few weeks. The silence in the hall was deep and unholy, and it jarred Obinna's nerves. The men stood still around him in the silence, and Obinna wondered what it all meant. To him, these men were very unserious jokers, but he was determined to cooperate with them to the end, just for the experience and the fun of it. He lifted up his eyes, made faces at them repeatedly, and scoffed silently at each of them. Then he lifted up his hands, folded his fingers into the *F.U. sign*, showed the sign to them, while contorting his face in an expression of profound contempt for them. But they all ignored him, and the silence persisted.

Then all ten figures, at a sign from Babatunde, suddenly began to chant in a strange, wild, ancient language, thus breaking the weird silence. The language was undecipherable to Obinna, or to anyone else, except to the chanters. On and on they chanted, for what seemed like several hours, until suddenly, the entire room was cast in very deep darkness. Then, as sudden as the darkness came, a mighty flood of bloody-red light illuminated the hall, followed by heavy smoke which billowed suddenly out of seeming nothingness. Pungent, sulphurous odour engulfed the entire hall. The ten hooded figures stopped chanting as they became intensely frightened. They all ran quickly to one corner of the hall where they crouched together, waiting and watching what was going on in horror. However, the unbelieving Obinna Kelechi remained seated on the stool where he was, and watched in amazement. A gasp escaped from some of the men as a shadowy, powerful and gigantic figure slowly took form in the midst of the fiery-red smoke.

As everyone in the room continued to watch the apparition in utmost fear, the immense figure that was slowly taking shape in the smoke materialized completely. And there he stood, the Prince of Darkness, or the Dark Angel himself, known more commonly as Satan, or Lucifer, the eternal spirit of evil. He emerged slowly from the midst of the smoke. His likeness was very much like that of man, but he was a lot fairer, taller, and statelier that his head was less than a foot from the ceiling; and behind him were his massive wings which spread out and folded repeatedly to the utter amazement and fascination of the onlookers. His entire aspect was intensely presumptuous and egotistic.

The moment he fully materialized, all the ten hooded figures fell down immediately on their faces, at his feet, in idolatrous worship of the gigantic figure of the Dark Angel which towered supremely over them all.

"Greetings, O Lucifer, son of the morning! Greetings, O Lucifer, Prince of Darkness! Greetings, O Lucifer, Master of the fates of all the damned! Greeting, O Lucifer, Master of all those on the road to perdition!" the men said repeatedly as they grovelled in fear at his feet.

"Arise!" He said in a rich sonorous voice, "Arise all of you, faithful servants of Lucifer, from the floor!"

The hooded men got up slowly to their feet.

The fallen Angel looked around him slowly, his huge pinions still flapping repeatedly behind him. His massive figure would project instant fear and dread into any human being who saw him.

Obinna watched the dark figure silently. There was a look of wonder and fear intermingled in his eyes, but not a word escaped his mouth. His face twitched terribly, his heart raced wildly; that at one point, he fell into a light faint, but revived almost instantly.

"Where is he on whose account the Dark Angel had been summoned hither?" The sonorous voice queried, "The one who seeks to be super-rich at the hands of the Dark Angel?"

Babatunde, the prime worshipper, pointed out Obinna.

The Dark Angel turned his attention to Obinna.

"Young man," he said, "What is thy name?"

"Obinna Kelechi," came the reply from Obinna in a somewhat strangulated voice.

"Thou seeketh great wealth and riches, as well as fame, at the hands of the Dark Angel; and all that shall the Dark Angel grant thee with many more fabulous things thou hast not requested. Thy wealth shall be without limits and without bounds; and with it thou shall have all other pleasures of life as much as thou desireth, but thou shalt enjoy all thy riches for only seven earth years! In exchange for thy wealth, I, the Dark Angel, also known as Lucifer, the proud and rebellious spirit, shall have thy Soul! At exactly the end of seven earth years, counting from this day, thou shall die, then shall I come, at the hour of thy death, to harvest thy Soul. Young man, will thou enter into this Pact with the Dark Angel?"

Obinna still looked on intensely bewildered but did not say anything.

THE PACT

"What manner of madness is all these?" He said to himself, "Why have I been surrounded by mad people for so long? Surely, I must be having another nightmare, or why should this imposing being materialize from seemingly nowhere and be talking about a Soul that does not even exist? Why should he even hint at such a nonentity? Certainly, I must be having a nightmare with Babatunde playing another leading role as he always did in my dreams! My life philosophy tells me correctly that there is no God, no Christ, and no devil, so who is this impostor who wants to make a deal with me? This must be another nightmare unquestionably! Life, according to my philosophy, begins at the time of conception and terminates with death. So, why should this terrific looking being be talking about a Soul that does not exist?"

"Young man," the colossal figure of the materialized spirit of evil repeated, "Wilt thou enter into this Pact with the Dark Angel?"

"Yes! Yes!!" Obinna screamed in response. He was feeling suddenly brave and very confident; and perhaps deluded that he was having yet another nightmare, he shouted again, "I enter into this Pact with you! If you can make me super-wealthy, super-rich and famous for seven years as you have hinted, if you really can, then in return, you can have the worthless thing you call a Soul!"

The evil Angel looked at him, but was silent momentarily.

"Dost thou sign and seal the Pact with me forever, young man?"

"Yes, yes," Obinna responded again as though overtaken by a fit of madness, "It is signed and sealed with you forever!"

"Very well," replied the Dark Angel, "I pronounce this Pact signed and sealed forever!"

Then he suddenly looked upwards with his great arms totally outstretched.

"I beckon on all the hosts of heaven and hell to witness the Pact!" The fallen Angel said very solemnly, "All immortal spirits, all elemental spirits, and all the spirits that inhabit the thousand billion worlds, I call on thee all to witness this day, the signing and sealing of the Pact, with the young man, Obinna Kelechi. His Soul is mine, and mine alone, from this day forward, forever and ever. No mortal Soul, or any entity here on the earth, or in the vast heavens above, or in the realm of fire in hell below, shall have the power to break the Pact!"

This pronouncement was followed by a dead, ominous silence.

"It is signed and sealed forever! The Pact between the mortal, Obinna Kelechi, and Lucifer, also known as Satan, the Proud and Rebellious Spirit of Evil, is signed and sealed forever! Lucifer, the son of the morning had spoken!"

At that very instant, a deafening thunderclap crashed violently, shattered a few windows in Babatunde's house, and shook the entire house fiercely to its very foundation. It was a sign given by the elemental spirits that were called to witness the diabolic Pact—that the Pact was indeed witnessed as signed and sealed.

"Very well," said the massive Angel, "My mission here is completed." Then he turned to Obinna, and said: "Young man, thou shall have thy deserts very shortly."

Then the fallen Angel turned slowly, looked at Babatunde, and addressed him.

"Faithful servant," he said, "Even as thou neareth the end of thy days on the earth, I shall be waiting to receive thy Soul home with me to the realms beyond; for three months only dost thou have left."

"Absolutely, Dark Lord." Babatunde replied with a sick smile and a deep bow.

A faint smile lit up the Dark Angel's face and without another word, he disappeared and was gone.

CHAPTER 15

Juliette had been very busy preparing for her wedding with Babatunde. She had travelled abroad severally to do her shopping and recently got back with Babatunde into the country from one of such trips. There was serious disagreement between them about where the venue of the wedding should be. She wanted to be wedded abroad—in the USA, or the UK—as was the practice of the super-rich in Nigeria, but Babatunde had objected sternly, and insisted that everything must take place within the country. Not wanting to flog the issue any further, she had succumbed reluctantly to his wishes. It appeared the plans and every other thing were going on smoothly and accordingly as planned. The wedding gown had been purchased in London, exquisitely designed specially for her; shoes had been bought—fine fitting shoes—the very best available that money could buy. The wedding cake was planned to be of gigantic proportions, to be designed in a way never seen before. Babatunde's suit had been ordered as well from abroad, and all the normal activities that characterized weddings had been taken care of to specific details. The reception would be held in Babatunde's house, and about two thousand guests had been invited. It was planned to be a grand wedding—one of its kind—that must be talked about for many months, or years, afterwards. The honeymoon had also been planned, a trip round the world, that would last for three months. The various luxurious hotels across the globe had been contacted, and reservations made.

However, one question remained. Which Church would they be wedded? This too had caused profound disagreement between them as Juliette wanted to be wedded normally in a Church, just like any other normal young woman would have wished, but apparently, she seemed to be unfamiliar yet with the quietly threatening and obstinate nature of her groom-to-be, Babatunde, who refused firmly, insisting that those who would wed them—the Pastor and his entourage—should perform the ceremony in his house. After much quarrels and arguments between them on this issue, Juliette, yet again in desperation, reluctantly agreed to Babatunde's wishes that the wedding vows and other related ceremonies should be performed in his house. Had her spiritual nature been more developed and more sensitive, perhaps she would have been able to discern, or perceive, the yearnings and promptings of her own Soul, warning her desperately in vain against entering into marriage with a man like Babatunde; warning her that she should walk away and flee forever from him while there was yet time. But Babatunde's riches and what she stood to gain were too much temptation for her. Had she been sensitive and receptive to her own Soul;

and obeyed its promptings, perhaps she would have escaped Babatunde's secret sinister plans, or reduced its grave magnitude.

Initially, it was not easy to find a Clergyman who was willing to perform the marital rites in the house. Eventually, the Pastor of an obscure Church in downtown Ikeja, after learning of the great affluence of the groom, and the promise of a bribe with a SUV, as well as of a substantial amount of cash, agreed to perform the marital ordinances in Babatunde's house.

This settled the last detail of the wedding, and the stage was set. What was left now was the waiting for the 30th of October, the date of the wedding which was still a month away.

II

Obinna Kelechi, since his initiation nearly three months ago, had changed tremendously. Enormous fortunes had simply flowed to him through various avenues some of which were not clear even to himself. He seemed to be attracting money the way a magnet attracts iron filings, he had developed the 'Midas touch' overnight, so it seemed to everyone who knew him, especially those who had known him for years. His confidence had soared tremendously, and so was his fame at home and abroad as an international business man. He had started a number of businesses some of which had spread abroad very quickly. Those businesses were literal money-spinners, rolling in large quantities of cash seemingly endlessly for him. He, who was desperately seeking to be employed about one year or so ago, was now an employer of over three thousand five hundred persons spread across the globe. He had travelled abroad with Monica to several countries on six occasions to take care of business, and for the mere pleasure of it. They had stayed in the best hotels in those countries, and enjoyed all the luxuries the hotels could offer.

On two occasions, he had been invited to stay in the host countries' presidential lodges with all the attached privileges. Currently, he was planning another trip with Monica.

He had been invited to dine with very powerful figures, royalties, highly-influential persons and politicians in some of the countries he had visited abroad. And even a Prime Minister, in one of the countries of the Middle East, had discussed some financial challenges facing his country with him, and pleaded earnestly with him for a possible loan to fix some of his country's most pressing problems. Obinna had obliged the Prime Minister without hesitation.

His hosts in some of the countries he had visited, even though he was always with Monica, would draw him aside, and whisper into his ears that in case he needed an additional female company for more deserving comfort, many would be at his disposal at the mere snap of his fingers. However, Obinna—being naturally disciplined—would simply smile and reply, "OK." But he had never asked, or snapped his fingers for that purpose. Perhaps it was out of respect for Monica, for there was no telling what he could do now in his new status as a very wealthy man had Monica not accompanied him on those trips.

Monica herself was no pushover when it came to sheer feminine beauty, charm and attractiveness as she was looking far lovelier and more voluptuous than ever. She could compete favourably with any woman, anywhere, in terms of flaunting her physical beauty, or in acts of coquetry. Many women had flashed their eyes bewitchingly at Obinna several times in public, or at gatherings, especially now with all his wealth, these episodes of furtive glances and flirtatious winking of the eyes from these women were more frequent. However, Monica's ever-presence at his side seemed to serve as an effective deterrent to these female admirers of his; and Monica herself would not hesitate to warn them strictly, if it became necessary, to steer clear of him; and let them know that the man, Obinna Kelechi, was taken and was not available to any other woman.

She had actually thanked God for giving her the courage to return to Obinna's life as she now had everything she had always wanted and more, and was now much happier than she had ever imagined. The money kept flowing in for them unceasingly and the flow seemed to come from an inexhaustible source. More so her former fiancé, the sixty-two year old widower, had suddenly passed away after a brief illness.

"So, I would have become a widow by now at so young an age," she had said to herself in a mixed emotion of regret and gratitude. "Thank God, I had the courage to leave him. May his Soul rest in peace."

III

However, Obinna, in his quiet moments—which were few indeed—was not really happy. His enormous wealth baffled him rather than made him happy. What happened that night at his initiation had challenged his little 'Philosophy of life' and shattered it completely.

He had since jettisoned that philosophy like a destructive bad habit, and had moved forward with his life, but at this very moment, he seemed confused and does not really know what to believe. Certainly, all the great wealth that had come to him in so short a time could not have happened naturally. Such vast amounts of wealth could not have come by chance. Rather, it confirmed Babatunde's assertion about the existence of a devil that was now manipulating everything in his favour. He himself had witnessed the materialization of the great fallen Angel during his initiation. This called for a serious pondering over for him.

"So there must be a Soul in existence?"

He would ask himself half-aloud and half-meditatively.

"And mine had been sold to the devil?"

He would ask himself half-affrightedly over and over again.

"Surely if a Soul exists and the devil also exists, then there must be a God also in existence somewhere,"

He would muse repeatedly.

He thought of Babatunde frequently. Their relationship had improved again after their bitter quarrel that day when Babatunde revealed the source of his wealth to him. After that unholy initiation ceremony, immediately the Dark Angel had disappeared, all the men in hood had lifted their hoods and congratulated him profusely, hugged him in turns, and welcomed him to the *Great Lucide'il Society*, the society or family of Lucifer. Babatunde was the first to hug and welcome him so effusively.

Oddly enough, Babatunde, in spite of the fact that he was the incumbent Chairman of the Society, had failed to invite any of the members of the Society to his forthcoming wedding. It was in one of the dailies that Obinna learned of the wedding. Was this an oversight, or was it deliberate? Could there be a reason for such an error of omission on the part of Babatunde, if indeed it was an error. Obinna was someone who never attended an occasion he was not invited. Thus, he had made up his mind not to attend the wedding unless Babatunde reached him, by whatever means, with an invitation even if it was just a few days to the wedding day. Only then would he and Monica attend.

What now terrified him was that the Dark Angel, now his lord and master, had given him only seven years to live. Thereafter he had proclaimed that Obinna would die, and he would be there to harvest his Soul. That statement, "Harvest thy Soul," as made by the Dark Angel, now frightened him, though initially he had been indifferent because of his unbelief at the time. If his Soul was really taken by the devil, then what would happen to it? Eternal damnation and punishment as he had been told and taught in the Churches several years ago? Could there really be a heaven or a hell as he was taught in Sunday school several years ago when he was still a young child growing up in Lagos? These and many other questions of this nature raced through his mind repeatedly.

His mind suddenly reverted to Martha. He had not seen her for a couple of months now, though he had called her and chatted with her twice on the telephone since the time they spent together at King-sized Delights. Any time he spoke with Martha on the phone, she always inspired the finer and better part of him. Her voice was always soothing to him, and he found himself still well-taken with her charms. He knew Martha would not care anything about his wealth; and he knew he could not depend or rely on his wealth to influence, or win her.

And what about Monica? Monica had brought up the issue of legalizing their relationship by getting married in Church. He had not given it much thought because he knew that at the back of his mind, it was Martha he really wanted; it was Martha he really loved. However, as it was not certain that he might ever be able to win Martha's heart; Monica was the next and only other woman he knew, as Monica herself had succeeded in blocking every other woman, very effectively, from getting intimate with him. Perhaps getting married to her would be worth giving a try. If he married

THE PACT

Monica, he knew it would be out of kindness to her, and not out of love. But he told himself he would give the matter more thought before he finally decided.

CHAPTER 16

It was October 30th, the long-awaited and over-hyped wedding day of Juliette and Babatunde had arrived at last. The wonderful-looking couple were gorgeously attired in their wedding apparels, and were standing with their parents who were also elegantly dressed in very rich native outfit. Juliette looked so lovely in her long, flowing, exquisitely-beautiful, wedding gown. Her face was excellently made up by professional make-up artists, that with her wedding gown, she looked almost angelic. Babatunde too was looking his very best, wearing an excellent black suit that costs almost a fortune in London. In their midst was the Pastor, also well-dressed, and smiling very happily. With him were his two assistants; and they all seemed very eager to administer the marital rites, and join the groom with his bride, so that the two can become one flesh, and proceed immediately on their honeymoon as they had both planned.

Babatunde's house was packed full to overflowing with guests. Two thousand guests had been invited, but there were probably three thousand, or more in the large house. This was not a problem anyway because there were more than enough food and drinks to entertain everyone present in the house several times over.

Soon, the marital vows were taken, rings exchanged, and Babatunde and Juliette were proclaimed Man and Wife by the Pastor. The marital kisses were also exchanged. The huge cake was cut, and the people were very excited and happy.

Five, live, musical bands had been hired to perform at the occasion, and the nuptial dance soon began. Juliette was extremely happy, happier than she had ever been in her life. This was obvious in the way she danced. She outdanced her new husband, without a doubt, by a very wide margin. Babatunde was a clumsy dancer, but he still managed to move his body a little bit, and exhibited a few dancing steps. Everyone clapped happily for the great dancing skills displayed by Juliette, and cheered her very excitedly by making a lot of noise. Then the guests came out to the dance floor, and joined the couple in dancing. The food and wine flowed ceaselessly, as the guests were fed to repletion, and the entire atmosphere was very gay and happy. Anyone who wanted more food or wine was never denied. After eating varieties of food several times over; some people stocked food into any container they could lay their hands on, and even into ridiculous places, to take home with them.

As the celebrations continued, Babatunde suddenly glanced at his wristwatch. The time was 11:58 am; then he took his bride by the hand, and they both sat down together. A look of concern suddenly appeared on his face. The place was still rowdy, and very noisy, with so much activities going on that nobody really noticed how deeply worried the groom had suddenly become. He looked at his wristwatch again, and it was just a few seconds to twelve noon. Immediately, he started sweating profusely.

Instinctively Juliette turned, just to admire him, but was instantly alarmed at how horribly pale he had become. When she saw the great amount of sweat streaming down his face, she knew something had gone very wrong with him. The wifely instinct prompted her instantly to bring out her scented, white handkerchief; to mop the sweat from his face.

"Honey, are you alright?" She asked him, utterly amazed as she mopped his face with the handkerchief, "Why are you"....

Poor, Juliette. She never completed that sentence, because suddenly, KKKAAABBBOOMMM!!!

A huge explosion suddenly rocked Babatunde's house, and the entire building was engulfed instantly in a wild conflagration! Babatunde and Juliette's body suddenly erupted into flames! Babatunde's house had suddenly turned into a veritable hell on earth with huge fires burning very fiercely, and dark smoke billowing consistently upwards and disappearing into the sky! The wedding scene quickly turned into a frenzied scene of intense chaos as people screamed violently, ran helter-skelter, and trampled upon one another as they tried to escape the raging inferno. Even those who attempted the escape were crushed to death by the flaming tall columns of the building which fell upon them. The nuptial music was instantly replaced by the deathly wailing sounds of the dying, the sounds of falling roofs, walls, shattering windows, falling huge pillars, and the peculiarly-horrifying sound made by the unrelenting and destructive fire itself, all intermingling very frightfully.

It was a horrific sight! Nothing so bad, nothing so cruel, nothing so destructive had ever been seen at a wedding ceremony in all the rich annals of this great city. The fire itself, exceedingly-vicious and absolutely-pitiless, spared no one. The bodies of the bride and groom were charred completely beyond recognition; so were that of their parents, the Pastor and his assistants, and numerous other persons. Some bodies had been roasted to death with articles of food such as beef, fish, chicken and rice still in their mouths. It was a stomach-churning sight, and yet an hour later, the fires still rage on. The entire area reeked with the odour of charred human flesh and blood. Over three thousand Souls had perished—burnt to their harrowing deaths—in this ill-fated wedding.

Many onlookers standing outside the building had immediately telephoned the Fire Service Department, but they were yet to arrive. Many bold ones amongst the onlookers attempted a brave rescue but the fires raged so badly that they were severely singed and had to abandon the effort, fearing for their own lives. Many of the onlookers stood helplessly watching and crying profusely at the sheer destruction. Some of them, in their profound misery, threw themselves recklessly on the ground and wept bitterly, rolling miserably on the bare ground—their misery, worsened perhaps by their inability to render any help to the screaming and dying victims. It was such a horrific sight. The forces of Darkness had wrought a wanton destruction of such astonishing magnitude as never witnessed before, and had wasted more than three thousand lives!

Some of the eyewitnesses, later, when interviewed, were willing to swear that they could make out the faint outlines of the figures of unearthly, gigantic, winged beings tearing down the walls of Babatunde's house in the inferno; pulling down its pillars, and had actually prevented the escape of those that would have been able to escape. They were willing to swear that those gigantic, winged beings actually started the fires in the first place and fuelled it to the finish. Whether or not these assertions were just a figment of the imaginations of these observers, none could really tell.

The fires continued to burn with unremitting fervour, and the dark, huge smoke continued to billow upwards relentlessly. The smell of burnt human bodies intensified so much that some of the eyewitnesses vomited severely while others retched loudly. From time to time, a large chunk of the building would fall, and at one stage, numerous currencies—nairas, dollars, pounds, euros, yens, rands—in large numbers were seen flying around the burning house. Some of them were already badly charred, and couldn't be spent; while others had escaped the fires. The wind carried some of these currencies, and landed them temptingly outside at the feet of onlookers.

"Don't touch the money! Don't touch the money!" cried somebody, "It is the devil's money!"

"It is tainted money," shouted another, "Don't touch it!"

"If you pick up this money, and spend it," explained another onlooker in a very loud voice while pointing at the notes, "It will bring a curse into your life! If you are rich, it will make you poor; and if you are poor, it will make you poorer and absolutely wretched!"

Thus, with warning statements like these being shouted repeatedly amongst the eyewitnesses; the monies, amounting to several millions in different currencies, were scattered everywhere on the ground, and no one attempted to pick up even one of them.

"I know the owner of this house!" cried another eyewitness, a woman, with tear-stained eyes. She pointed at Babatunde's burning house as she spoke, "I know him quite well because I live just a few blocks away. He practises devilry and black magic! At times, he disturbs the entire neighbourhood with weird, hellish sounds that emanate from this building, sounds that chill us all, his neighbours, to the marrow, especially at night. The judgement of heaven has come upon him at last, I always knew his days were numbered!"

Thereafter, the Fire Service with their loud sirens eventually arrived the scene in their huge fire trucks to pick up the pieces. After struggling with the fire for about four hours, it was ultimately subdued.

Joshua Anjorin Babatunde's once magnificent and much-envied house now lay in absolute ruins. It was levelled completely to the ground by the angry inferno. Every available space on the ground was strewn with burnt dead bodies, most of them, charred beyond recognition. Emergency service workers had been called to evacuate the bodies for mass burial. Even as these workers worked ceaselessly to evacuate the bodies, some hateful scavenger birds could be seen already circling the scene of the carnage hoping to make a feast out of a very pathetic situation. The entire nation was thrown into severe mourning when the news of what happened at the wedding had circulated round the country.

II

Martha initially fainted when she heard that her friend, Juliette, was no more. When she revived, she cried uncontrollably, and could not be comforted; not even her dearly-beloved parents could console her. Perhaps it was out of the knowledge that she narrowly missed the wedding, and would have been one of the victims. She had been spared a similar fate suffered by those who attended the wedding. Although she had resolved never to set foot again in Babatunde's house, several months ago, after the way she was scolded by Juliette the last time she was there; however, she and Juliette had remained, more or less, friends. When they fixed the date of the wedding, and Juliette invited her, she decided to attend just out of her desire to please Juliette.

However, she was warned very sternly by an unseen voice in a dream to steer clear of Babatunde's house on the 30th of October. Fearing she would permanently lose Juliette's friendship if she did not attend, she prepared to go in spite of the warning. Then, strangely enough, her car would not start. After about an hour later of trying to start the car with the assistance of a mechanic without success; the mechanic left with the intention of returning to tow the car away. However, immediately the mechanic left, the car suddenly roared back to life when Martha turned the key again. Soon after the car had started, an urgent telephone call from the Abbess of the Franciscan Convent demanded her presence immediately in one of the Orphanages Martha personally catered for. The Abbess informed Martha that one of her beloved orphans was dying and needed urgent medical attention. Her car was needed to take the young child to the hospital immediately. Martha had to make a quick choice: Juliette's wedding, or the life of her beloved orphan? She chose to save the life of the orphan, and immediately drove to the Orphanage to take the child to the hospital. In her thoughts, she told herself she would plead with Juliette to understand her situation, and would make it up to her by getting her a fantastic wedding present. Then the next thing she heard was the heartbreaking news that everybody at the wedding had perished in a mysterious and catastrophic fire outbreak. Juliette's death completely broke her heart that she could not do anything for several days afterwards. In her profound grief, she prayed constantly for the repose of the Soul of her friend, Juliette, and her husband, Babatunde, as well as the other hapless victims at the ill-fated wedding.

Obinna Kelechi was absolutely devastated when he learnt of the horrifying deaths of Babatunde and Juliette as well as thousands of their guests at the wedding reception. He was so disturbed that he could not attend to any business activity for a few days. When he recovered a little from his depression, he began to think and ask himself questions.

"Was the accident at the wedding a deliberately planned occurrence? Could that be the reason why Babatunde had deliberately excluded members of the Society from the wedding, to protect them from being killed, knowing full well that each of the members also have their own day with the devil?"

Certainly, Obinna reasoned, Babatunde knew his time was up; he knew he was going to die soon. Obinna could still recall very clearly that the Dark Angel had conversed briefly with Babatunde on that memorable day of his own initiation into the Society, and reminded Babatunde that he had just three months left on earth. Obinna had also wondered why Babatunde would be preparing to get married when he knew his death was so close at hand. Perhaps the carnage at the wedding was orchestrated after all, Obinna mused.

"But how horrifying!" He said aloud, "To take a person like the lovely and promising Juliette whose life was still stretched out far ahead of her, and numerous others, to their untimely deaths, was selfish and wicked to say the least."

Many newspapers had already carried it in their headlines, and hinted that perhaps the forces of Darkness had something to do with the catastrophe at the wedding. That reminded Obinna of the forthcoming meeting of the *Great Lucide'il Society* members in a week's time. He believed that at the Meeting, each of the members would reveal his opinion of what actually happened at the wedding, and a new Chairman would be elected, or selected, as the case might be.

Chapter 17

The years rolled by very quickly and nothing eventful happened except that Obinna and Monica were now legally married. They were not wedded in Church as Obinna's conscience would not allow him because he knew the Agreement he had made with the forces of Darkness. Though Monica had pressured him repeatedly for a Church wedding; he always assured her, they would bless their marriage in Church later. However, Monica had no inkling that her husband was somehow mixed up with evil forces, and that he was not even confident enough of setting his foot in a Church.

Obinna, now worth billions, was not a happy man in spite of all his money. At times, in secret, after much thinking and worrying, he would suddenly start crying very profusely. He would wake up at night, and leave his bed very quietly, taking great care not to wake up his wife, and hide himself in one of the other rooms of his house, just to cry. He was slowly losing his mind, so it seemed. There was a huge emptiness, or gulf, in his Soul. His Soul longed for something more; something far beyond mere riches, or wealth. Something was definitely missing in his life. He reminisced frequently on his past, when he had nothing. He actually wished he had the mental peace he had back then. Though he suffered physically at the time, but now, he was in constant mental, emotional and spiritual torment, which in his own opinion, was far worse than all the physical sufferings he ever endured when he had no money. Now, he was constantly in mental agony. He never recalled himself crying at any time when he was poor, but now, despite all his wealth, he cried virtually everyday, deep anguished cries on most days and every night. At times, he and Monica would deliberately take long trips abroad, just to keep his mind occupied and not give it the opportunity to grieve so much. What was even more common with him at the time was that he hardly got a restful sleep at night. His sleep, whenever he was lucky to get one, was always troubled by dreams and visions of fiends and evil spirits who consistently mocked him, or chased him around in his dreams. At times, he would suddenly scream in his sleep at night, severely terrified, waking up Monica who would instantly reach out for him, hold him tenderly to her bosom, while praying for his peace of mind. At other times, those dreams take the form of his own funeral service with fiends as guests, and fiends officiating. Then the funeral service would suddenly end with a wild and terribly harsh rancorous laughter by the officiating fiend. One day, he was willing to swear that he distinctly heard the same laughter after he was already fully awake from sleep. No doubt that he was now the victim of the taunts, ridicules and wiles of demons.

As his wealth grew, so was the depression that oppressed his Soul. After all he had been through, he now believed very strongly in the existence of the Soul. He now believed indeed in the immortality of the Soul. From time to time, he thought of Babatunde, and the horrifying way he had died. Would he end up that same way? He cringed at the mere thought of it. This was the fifth year since his initiation, thus mathematically, he still had two years to live. He calculated the exact date he was expected to die, using the date of his initiation as reference point, and arrived at July 28. Thus, by July 28, in two years' time, he should have kept his house in order before the devil came to take him away. He was terrified, not because he was afraid to die, but of what would happen to his Soul after death.

The Dark Angel, with whom he had entered into a demonic Pact, with his Soul as wager, does not know what the words, "Pity," or

THE PACT

"Mercy," meant. His looks were absolutely cruel, pitiless and egotistic. There was absolutely no way he could meet the Dark Angel in a middle path! The famed Middle Path Philosophy, he reasoned, would not work with the Dark Angel.

He thought about his wife, Monica. She wanted to have children, and this he understood, was a normal desire of most married women in the Nigerian society. Secretly, he hoped that no child would bless their marriage as he knew that the child, or children, as the case might be, would very quickly become fatherless since he had just two years left to live. He wondered how Monica would cope after his demise. She would probably remarry, and move on with her life after her memory of him would have dimmed or faded. He had actually learned to love her genuinely now—as Monica herself had boldly predicted on her return into his life—that he sincerely does not want to see her suffer in any way. He really preferred that she remarried after his death, realize her dream of having children elsewhere, and continue with her life as she was still relatively young. Though Monica had a good education, and was a University graduate, he wondered if she would be able to manage his numerous estates and vast businesses after his death, or would those businesses and the wealth she would inherit from him bring the forces of darkness into her life? Better for the wealth and businesses to crumble and go down the drain than to make his wife the prey of satanic forces! That was unthinkable for him. This was his conclusion on the issue of his bequest. However, he knew he would never be able to bring himself to tell her about what he had done, and the kind of Agreement he had signed and sealed with evil forces.

He had been avoiding the members of the *Great Lucide'il Society* for some time now, preferring to be alone rather than be with them. He wondered if the other members of the Society were having similar experiences as he; or was his case peculiar? They all seemed very happy, gay and highly successful men, or were they also suffering in secret? He could not answer these questions as none of them had ever admitted any unusual occurrence in their lives. He also wondered how many years they had been given to live after their initiations. He later learned that most of the members got between twenty-five to thirty years after their initiations. This made him more depressed as he felt that the Dark Angel was very unfair to him, to have given him only seven years, the least time amongst all of them. Why this unfairness to him? He had no idea.

His thought suddenly shifted to Martha. Martha was now, more or less, a family friend as he had invited her to witness his legal wedding with Monica three years ago in a court. Monica liked Martha the instant she met her, and they had been relating very well like great friends. Strangely enough, Monica never suspected that he, Obinna, her husband, had been a secret admirer of Martha, and had even preferred Martha to her. After the Legal wedding that day, before she left, Martha had strolled quietly to his side, looking as beautiful as ever.

"Won't you also marry her in Church?" She had said to him in her typical, attractive voice, "I think you should, Mr. Obinna, to make your union with her acceptable and holy before God."

He could not really reply her. He merely gazed emptily into her beautiful eyes; that was all he did in response.

Should he call Martha and tell her everything? Perhaps she might be able to help him as Martha seemed to be the only sane, decent and faithful adherent of the Christian Faith that he knew. He wrestled with this thought in his mind for several months; and any time he considered it, everything within him seemed to rise up against him, and even the very air and the walls around him, seemed to find voices, all combining to mock him intensely for considering such a cowardly, silly and ridiculous decision. Nevertheless, after a great effort of the Will, one day, he forced himself and eventually called Martha on the phone. Martha sounded pleasantly surprised to receive his call.

"Why, Mr. Obinna," she had said playfully, "I expected your wife to be the only one calling me now, and no longer you. Please, don't hurt her feelings by making her suspicious, or jealous, because she is such a wonderful woman."

Obinna apologized to her.

"Please, Martha," he pleaded with her, "I need to see you urgently, not in my house, as I don't want to let my wife to know about it."

"Look, Mr. Obinna," began Martha, a little sternly, "I cannot agree to that. Things between us have changed with your status as a married man now, and your wife is my friend. Do you even realize the kind of scandalous and malicious rumour that could spread if anyone who knew either of us spotted us together in public?"

"I know, I know," Obinna said repeatedly with an urgent tone in his voice, "But this is very important to me, Martha, please."

"I'm sorry, Mr. Obinna. I am really very sorry that I'll have to disappoint you, no matter how important the issue you want to discuss with me. I'll talk with you only in the presence of your wife," Martha insisted.

This was followed by a long pause.

"Martha," Obinna addressed her by name in an ominously quiet voice, "You must help me now because this is a matter beyond life and death as I've sold my Soul to the devil."

Chapter 18

Martha was seated directly opposite Obinna in one of Obinna's yet unrented apartments located in one of his numerous estates. She was crying with copious amounts of tears flowing from her eyes, down her lovely face, to get sucked into her beautiful, cream-coloured dress, creating faint patterns on the dress. She tried drying the tears severally, but they kept flowing unrestrained that her two handkerchiefs were thoroughly drenched with her tears.

Obinna focused his eyes on her. He was secretly admiring her again, for Martha was blessed naturally with real beauty—inner and outer beauty combined—almost divine in its very essence. Her Soul and heart were pure; her nature was very sympathetic, kind and patient. All these features, in addition to her angelic face, made her a veritable Angel in human flesh.

Obinna thought she looked even lovelier in her grief. After the last time they communicated on the phone, and Martha had refused to see him in private; Obinna, left with no option, had simply let the cat out of the bag by letting her know how grave the matter was, and telling her point blank on the telephone that he had sold his Soul to the devil, and that he needed her help desperately. When she heard what he had said, she suddenly felt as though she was in a dream, or a trance, for a few moments. What kind of talk was that? She had asked herself as she had never heard of anything like that, the selling of one's Soul to the devil! When she recovered herself from the trance-like state, and realizing the incredible gravity of the matter, she quickly agreed to see him, and requested for the address of the place he had chosen for the clandestine meeting. He then described the housing estate and apartment to her, somewhere in Yaba, in great details.

Obinna was already waiting for her when she got there. Without wasting time, he told her the entire story from the very beginning: when and how he first met Babatunde; the time of his initiation into the satanic *Great Lucide'il Society*; the immediate change in his fortunes afterwards; the constant torment by evil spirits, especially at night, to the present day. He held absolutely nothing back. These were the reasons for Martha's unremitting tears and grief.

At last, she struggled and controlled herself.

"I always knew Babatunde was somehow involved in evil," she said tearfully. "The first time Juliette took me to his house to meet him; instantly, something within me warned me about him, told me to keep my distance from him."

This was followed by a prolonged pause.

"So Babatunde was really responsible for Juliette's death, and the deaths of all those people at the wedding?" She asked him, still very tearful.

"Yes," he replied.

Then she broke into another bout of tears. However, a short while later, she struggled again and controlled herself.

"Mr. Obinna," she said, "Remember I warned you about him that day we were out together in Ikeja."

She paused here again to wipe fresh tears away from her eyes.

"Perhaps, Mr. Obinna," she resumed tearfully, "If you had listened to me then, and had taken your leave of him, these horrible things you told me about wouldn't have happened to you."

"I know, Martha, I know," Obinna said regretfully, "I wish I had listened to you, then, Martha. But, please, Martha, what can you possibly do to help me now seeing the mistake had been made already?"

"I am still stunned that you actually saw Satan materialize, Mr. Obinna. Everything seemed so surreal to me now, perhaps I need some time to grasp the details of everything you've told me, Mr. Obinna, and digest them properly, please."

Obinna watched as two tears suddenly flowed downwards from both of her eyes to her chest. He thought that such sympathy, such love, as she had the capacity to feel and show were rare indeed amongst mortals. He allowed himself to become distracted again by admiring her secretly.

"What an excellent wife Martha would have made for any man," he thought. "But perhaps no man on earth deserved her, she seemed too tidied up, too neat and too clean for this world," he concluded.

"I'll speak to my Parish Priest!" Martha said at last, her voice still tearfully shaky, "His name is Rev. Fr. John Michaels. He is Northern Irish by birth but a naturalized Nigerian. He is a wonderfully-gifted and world-famous Exorcist. I'll tell him the entire story as you have related it to me, Mr. Obinna. If any human being can help you, I believe he's the one. I feel he can liberate you from the evil forces that dominate your life now, and perhaps, break the Pact you made with the devil. He recently returned from Belfast where he travelled to perform an exorcism."

"Help at last is on the way," Obinna quietly said with a huge sigh of relief.

This was followed by a short silence.

"Martha," Obinna said, "I hope you now understand why I'm keeping this a secret from my wife, because the moment she understands the situation, it will break her down completely, and make her very ill—mentally, physically and emotionally ill—perhaps mortally ill, because she is so delicately constituted."

Martha nodded in understanding.

"I'll keep you informed," she told him, "Of my meeting with Rev. Fr. John Michaels."

Then she stood up slowly, and asked to be excused to leave. Obinna stood up too, and walked with her to the door. Then he said goodbye to her, and watched her through the window as she drove away. A flicker of hope was beginning to shine in his heart; suggesting to him that, perhaps, there's a way out of the imbroglio he had entangled himself in with the devil.

II

The next morning, Martha attended morning Mass at St. Christopher's Cathedral. Immediately after the Mass, she ran after Rev. Fr. John Michaels, and soon caught up with him, as he turned towards his residential suites.

"Please, Father Michaels!" she called out to him, "I'll like to see you, sir."

The kindly old priest heard her, turned around, and smiled instantly.

"Alright, Sister Martha," he said, "Do you want me to bless your new rosary for you?"

"No, Father." She responded as she did her obeisance, "It's way more than that."

"Alright, talk to me, Martha. What is the problem?"

"It's not what we can discuss out here, Father. Can you, please, grant me a little of your time in your office, sir?"

"When?"

"Father, if possible, right now because it is very urgent."

"Right now?"

"Yes, right now."

This was followed by a short moment of hesitation by the Priest.

"Alright," Rev. Fr. John Michaels said eventually, "Go and wait for me in my office. I'll be with you in fifteen minutes."

"Thank you, Father."

Martha turned, and headed straight for Rev. Fr. John Michaels office, whilst he proceeded to his residential suites.

III

Exactly fifteen minutes later, the Priest was seated at his desk with Martha who sat directly opposite him in his office. He asked her why she wanted to see him. Then Martha, with tears streaming from her eyes, narrated the entire story about Obinna Kelechi to the Priest.

He did not interrupt her, but waited patiently for her to finish.

"What is your relationship with this man?" He asked her when she had finished telling the story.

"A friend," she replied calmly.

"Be comforted, my daughter," he told her very kindly with a smile. "Dry those tears of yours, and be not afraid."

Then he smiled confidently again, a very reassuring smile.

"I'm yet to encounter any accursed demon of hell that I'm unable to cast out," he told her his old hackneyed catch phrase that had characterized him over the years.

Martha relaxed, and was hopeful with the confident utterances of the Priest. Given his world-famous achievements at driving out devils, breaking spells, and reversing curses, Martha felt completely reassured.

"When can I see him?" He asked her suddenly.

"As soon as it is convenient for you, sir."

"Let me prepare for seven days," he told her. "In seven days' time, come in the morning, after Mass, and take me to him."

"Seven days from now is Friday, sir." Martha said quietly.

"Precisely," responded Rev. Fr. Michaels.

"Thank you, very much, sir."

"You're welcome, my daughter."

Thereafter, he pronounced a benediction on her. Then Martha stood up, thanked him, and left the Cathedral somewhat in a hurry to catch up with work.

IV

Six days passed quickly and uneventfully. The seventh day was Friday; and in the morning, as planned, Martha, Rev. Fr. John Michaels and two of his assistants were with Obinna at his apartment in Yaba. Obinna was lying very still, on his back, in the bed with both eyes closed, though he was fully conscious and somewhat nervous. The only visible sign of movement in him were the occasional twitches of his facial muscles. The exorcism was set to commence, and the Parish Priest, Rev. Fr. John Michaels, told Martha quietly to excuse them from the room.

"This is no scene for anyone not familiar with exorcism to witness," he told her nicely.

"Alright, Father," Martha replied obediently.

She left the room, and went to wait prayerfully in one of the other rooms in the apartment.

Then the exorcism started. Indistinct weird sounds reached Martha where she knelt down in prayer in the adjacent room. The sound later became louder, and reached her ears distinctly, but she struggled, tried her best not to concentrate on the mysterious and meaningless sounds. She continued in prayer, with closed eyes, and on her knees, for the support of Rev. Fr. John Michaels and his helpers.

After about three hours had passed; a sudden, loud, horrendous sound was heard. Rev. Fr. Michaels was abruptly lifted up from the floor and hurled out of the room where the exorcism was being performed by a sudden, vicious force. He was flung violently through the closed door, thus breaking the door completely. Thereafter, the whole house shook vigorously, and the room became filled with fiery-red smoke and pungent sulphurous odour. The sudden sound almost made Martha to pass out where she knelt down in the next room. However, she struggled; and continued with her prayers.

Rev. Fr. John Michaels sustained very severe head and back injuries, and had lost consciousness instantly. His assistants came running out of the room severely terrified. They screamed repeatedly and called on the name of Jesus Christ, to protect them from evil. These men, for the first time in their lives, had just set their eyes on the physical form of the devil himself!

Obinna, severely frightened by the sudden sound and all the commotion, had curiously opened his eyes very slowly. What he saw filled him instantly with dread as his eyes rested upon the massive, terrifying figure of the Dark Angel who stood staring at him on the bed in utter disgust. He sneered menacingly at Obinna, reminded him very sternly that the Pact, which he had signed and sealed with him, remained binding forever! He reminded Obinna that no physical, or spiritual force; or any entity, anywhere, had the power to break it! The Dark Angel warned him not to deceive himself again by trying to wriggle out of the Pact, because there was no way out! Rather, he advised Obinna to live up like a real man, and enjoy the little time he still had left on earth. The materialized spirit of evil further reminded him that he, Lucifer, had kept his own part of the Pact, and lavished him with billions of money, far more than he could ever spend in his lifetime. It was binding on Obinna, also, to keep his own part of the Pact, or Agreement. Thus was Obinna warned, rebuked, by the fallen Angel. Thereafter, he vanished from the room as sudden as he had appeared, just like a puff of air.

V

The entire Christian community was thrown into severe mourning when it learnt of the death of Rev. Fr. John Michaels, the most senior Parish Priest and Pastor of St. Christopher's Cathedral, at the age of seventy-two years. However, the real cause of his death was concealed from the public as the Church reasoned that it could bring a smear on the name of Jesus Christ. However, the Catholic community in Northern Ireland were given the full details and circumstances of his death. They seemed satisfied with the explanation, as they were familiar with the daring nature of the Priest. They knew he was not afraid of any challenge, and would engage even the devil himself, in a fisticuff, if it became necessary. The burial rites were performed without delay, and he was buried in the Cathedral crypt as he had previously instructed a few days prior to his death as though he foresaw his own death.

Meanwhile, Martha was absolutely devastated, distraught and overwrought with grief, feeling very guilty of the death of Rev. Fr. John Michaels.

"After all," she had said regretfully and repeatedly to herself amidst unending tears, "I was the one who involved the Priest in the event that led to his death."

She thus, very unforgivingly, chastised herself continually to the extent that she became completely incapacitated at work. However, she was finally consoled by the entire elders and leaders of the Christian community who met with her in a special Meeting, and explained in very clear terms, that the blame was not hers. They explained that Rev. Fr. John Michaels knew very well that he was going to die in his attempt to break an unbreakable Pact, from the various statements he had made during the seven days he prepared for the titanic encounter with Lucifer. He had been warned in a vision that he would die if he attempted to break a Pact that had been signed and sealed as unbreakable by any mortal, spirit, or force anywhere; a Pact that was witnessed by the immortal spirits! However, in spite of the grim warning of this dream, the Priest was undeterred.

"I will fight the devil with my last breath, and liberate the children of God he had chained in bondage," he was quoted to have said several times while he prepared by fasting and prayer.

It was after this Meeting with the elders of the Church that somewhat comforted Martha. As the Priest was laid six feet beneath the earth in a casket in the Church crypt; Martha, a little recovered from her profound grief, but still sorely in tears, stood alone by the Priest's graveside, praying very earnestly.

"Rev. Fr. John Michaels," she said finally, "May your gentle Soul rest in perfect peace at the bosom of our Lord Jesus Christ, Amen."

CHAPTER 19

Few weeks later, after the burial of Rev. Fr. John Michaels, and as life was returning gradually to normal for many of the most affected persons by the sudden and painful demise of the Parish Priest; somewhere in Yaba, in the same apartment where the Priest had been killed while attempting to liberate Obinna from the bondage of the Pact, was Martha seated with Obinna. He had invited her there again for two reasons. Firstly, to express how sorry he was to her for the late Parish Priest who had lost his life while trying to deliver him, and also to find out from her what next could possibly be done for him towards his liberation from the throes of the forces of darkness.

"I'm doomed for eternity!" He suddenly broke into tears as they discussed, "No hope for me, but eternal damnation in the fires of hell!"

Martha watched him with sympathy, but she did not say anything.

"If the greatest Exorcist on the planet could not help me," he whined tearfully, "But died while trying, then my case is absolutely hopeless!"

Martha started sobbing too, for his tears had induced hers. She tried to encourage him quietly, but Obinna would not be encouraged, he was entirely despondent and hysterical with trepidation.

Eventually, after some minutes, he stopped crying and dried his tears. Martha calmed down too, and the two of them just sat in the silence for a while, not saying anything. Thereafter, Martha suddenly broke the silence.

"The name of the new Parish Priest," she said somewhat meditatively, "Is Rev. Fr. Emmanuel Oluwatosin. He will be here tomorrow to perform the Sacrament of Baptism for you, Mr.

Obinna. I discussed with him before I came here, and he agreed to come with me tomorrow and administer the Sacrament to you."

He nodded his head quietly in appreciation and gratitude to her for all her efforts in helping him. The Sacrament of Baptism? He does not really know what that meant. But given his situation, he would gladly try out anything suggested to him by someone like Martha, provided it had the possibility of helping him in anyway.

"Try not to worry overmuch, Mr. Obinna," Martha said to him reassuringly, "I believe there are no circumstances on this earth, however seemingly difficult, that is impossible with God."

Martha stood up after that statement, and prepared to leave. He thanked her again for all her care and concern about him. Then he assured her that he would be there tomorrow to await the new Parish Priest of the Cathedral.

II

The following morning, two cars—a *Hyundai Elantra* and a *Mercedes Benz*— pulled up in front of the gates of a housing estate in Yaba. Two security personnel emerged from their duty post and stared at the cars.

"What do you want?" One of them asked.

"Good morning," Martha greeted them from the *Hyundai,* "We wish to see, Mr. Obinna Kelechi."

"Alright." They replied. Then after a sketchy search of both cars, the men opened the gates for them.

Both cars entered the estate, the *Hyundai* preceding the *Benz,* and stopped right in front of one of apartments in the estate. The door of the apartment opened; and Obinna Kelechi, looking worn with worry, came out. On sighting the cars, especially the *Hyundai,* which he knew belonged to Martha, he waved at them immediately.

The door of the *Hyundai* opened, and Martha, looking as lovely as ever, stepped out.

"Good morning, Mr. Obinna," she said to him somewhat cheerfully.

"Good morning, Martha," he responded rather gloomily. Then he added, "Thanks for coming."

Martha held the door of the *Benz* open, and three Priests, all dressed in canonicals, alighted.

"Mr. Obinna," Martha addressed him, "Please, meet Rev. Fr. Emmanuel Oluwatosin, the new Parish Priest and Pastor of the Cathedral." She also introduced the other Priests to him as Rev Fr. Christian Uduak and Rev. Fr. Pascal Ikechukwu. "This is Mr. Obinna Kelechi," she told the Priests, "He's the one on whose account we're here."

Rev. Fr. Emmanuel Oluwatosin was an averagely tall man, dark in complexion, and around sixty years of age. His other colleagues with him were younger by ten to fifteen years. After the brief introduction by Martha, he turned to Obinna with an encouraging smile.

"Martha has told me everything about you," he said to Obinna, "But I want you to know that all you need is an unshakable faith in God to defeat Satan and his wiles. It is in our darkest moments that we need to trust God the most, though circumstances around us might make that almost impossible for us. But, have no fear, Mr. Obinna, for Jesus Christ, our Lord and Saviour, has paid the price for all your sins and your indiscretions in regard to the Pact."

"Thank you, Father," Obinna muttered. "Please, let's go inside the house, sir."

He held the door open for them, and they all entered.

III

Obinna led them to a large room. Without wasting time, Rev. Fr. Emmanuel Oluwatosin commenced immediately with the ceremony. Holy Water was sprinkled at all corners of the room for sanctification purposes, and incense was burned in a censer. This was followed by a session of prayers and praises to the Most High God. Thereafter, Obinna was made to kneel in their midst. Then he was sprinkled with Holy water. The ceremony continued in the form of questions from the Priest to which Obinna responded affirmatively as thus:

"You, Obinna Kelechi, do you reject Satan?"

"I do."

"Do you reject all the works of Satan?"

"I do."

"And all his empty promises?"

"I do."

"Do you believe in God, the Father Almighty, the Creator of Heaven and Earth?"

"I do."

"Do you believe in Jesus Christ, His only Son, Our Lord, who was born of the Virgin Mary, was crucified, died and was buried but rose from the dead, and is now seated at the right hand of the Father?"

"I do."

"Do you believe in the Holy Spirit, the Holy Catholic Church, the Communion of the Saints, the Forgiveness of Sins, the Resurrection of the Body, and the Life Everlasting?"

"I do."

"God, the all-powerful Father of our Lord Jesus Christ has given you, Obinna Kelechi, a New Birth by Water and the Holy Spirit, and forgiven all your sins. May He also keep you faithful to our Lord Jesus Christ for ever and ever."

"Amen."

This concluded the ceremony. As the soon the rites ended, Obinna felt as though a heavy burden had been lifted from his heart. He felt really free for the first time in many years. Immense joy just seemed to flow into his heart from nowhere. Thereafter, he became ecstatic. Then with profuse tears streaming down his eyes, He screamed, "I believe in God! I believe in Jesus Christ, His Son! I believe in the Holy Spirit! I believe in the Immaculate Conception of Jesus Christ! I believe that He died, resurrected, and I believe He will come again in glory! I believe! I believe! I believe! I believe! I believe!"

He just couldn't contain the joy that welled up so suddenly and enormously in his heart. On and on he went, whether on his knees on the floor, or lying facedown, or faceup, he just kept on yelling, as the warm tears continued to flow, that he now believed in God.

When he eventually ceased and calmed down, Rev. Fr. Emmanuel Oluwatosin, almost tearfully, with the two other Priests with him, and Martha, already in tears of joy, welcomed Obinna into the family of the children of God. Thereafter, Obinna departed with them for the Cathedral where an aggressive Christian teaching and counselling program was instantly instituted for him. He was tutored directly for several weeks by Rev. Fr. Emmanuel Oluwatosin himself. He took him under his wing, accepted him as he would a son, tutored him directly for several weeks until every question about God that had plagued Obinna's mind for several years was satisfactorily answered in the light of the Holy Scriptures and the Gospels of Jesus Christ.

During the course of the program, Obinna became an enthusiastic Christian of the Catholic Faith. It was inferred earlier that immediately after the Baptismal rites, his long-lost peace of mind returned. It is also important to point out here that in addition to his peace of mind which he regained, no longer was he troubled in his dreams by yelling and screaming fiends at night. His nightly cries also ceased altogether. He attended Church regularly, and together with his wife, was administered the Sacrament of Matrimony after fulfilling the necessary conditions. Thus, they both became very zealous members of the Cathedral. Obinna Kelechi felt exactly like a man from whose shoulders a crushing weight had been lifted suddenly.

Martha saw him and his wife, Monica, regularly at the Cathedral during Mass. And no one could possibly guess, or fathom, the sheer pleasure and joy that Martha now had in her gentle heart and spirit; just to see Obinna and his wife amongst the family of God's children in the Church. This was her sincere wish for him, from the very moment they got acquainted, a wish that had finally become a reality for her.

IV

Another year passed rapidly and uneventfully except that Obinna and his wife grew steadily in their knowledge of God and His son, Jesus Christ. They both read and studied the Bible together with the same fervour a starving man or woman would eat a nice, nourishing meal. But he still kept a secret from her, the secret of his past involvement with the forces of evil. He just couldn't bring himself to tell her. However, he hoped that someday, somehow, she would learn the truth by herself.

Eventually, the 28th of July came, Obinna's seventh year from the day he was initiated, and the day he was expected to die. He felt unwell and suddenly developed a slight headache that night. He was fully aware that that night was perhaps his last night, so, very quietly, he rose from his bed, taking great care not to wake his wife, and, entered another room, shut and bolted the door. However, he was not afraid of anything; for he had profound peace in his heart now, "The peace of God, which passeth all understanding," held sway in his heart. He was ready to meet with death, confidently, without fear or anxiety. He suddenly became aware of a presence, as though he was being watched by unseen eyes, but he was unafraid. He made the sign of the cross, said a short prayer, and laid down on the bed. He soon fell asleep in the room, and while in that sleep, he slipped slowly into unconsciousness. Thereafter, he started drifting slowly away in death.

Outside, not far from the room where Obinna was dying, the Dark Angel, or Lucifer, waited, with a host of demons with him, just as he had said he would, to Obinna at his initiation, for the purpose of harvesting his Soul. They waited unperceived, without a single sound, they waited patiently until Obinna eventually gave up the ghost. Then very swiftly, the Dark Angel and his host, approached the bed where Obinna's Soul was. However, before they could reach where the Soul lingered, a sudden blinding flash of light was cast very fiercely upon them, and a powerful deafening sound, as of a mighty trumpet blowing, was heard behind them.

Immediately, the Dark Angel turned to see what was happening. What he saw caused his heart to fail him completely, and he became utterly dismayed, as his eyes beheld, not a human being, but—the Prince of Peace, the Holy one of God, the Saviour of the World, in His full glory—Jesus Christ, the Son of the Living God!

Chapter 20

Jesus Christ—the Son of God and Saviour of the world—stood in the clouds, tall, majestic, grand, superb and supreme! He was covered in a glittering spotlessly white garment from His neck down to His feet; and from His splendid brow were reflected all the glories of eternity! His face and form were infinitely beautiful beyond description by mortal mouth or pen; not once had any mortal eyes beheld such supernal beauty, such awesome glory. His hair was as white as wool, and upon his head was a golden crown on which was written, "King of Kings and Lord of Lords." His head was encircled by a majestic, mystical radiance with a hue unlike anything ever seen on the earth. The sheer splendour and grandeur around the Saviour was absolutely incredible and utterly awe-inspiring.

A mighty wind started blowing; bending all trees, shrubs, grasses, in total adoration to the Saviour. Then came the sound of many rushing waters: the seven seas, with their rivers, and together with the winds, mysteriously whooshed the words:

"HOSANNA TO THE SON OF DAVID. BLESSED IS HE THAT COMETH IN THE NAME OF THE LORD, HOSANNA IN THE HIGHEST!"

As the words rippled through the atmosphere, the vibrations were picked up by the mountains, the hills, the valleys and the plains, and they all echoed it, in a most terrifying manner, very loudly and repeatedly amongst themselves, causing the words to reverberate to the very ends of the earth and penetrating far into space. As the words resonated everywhere, an ear-splitting thunder suddenly rents the night, and lightning flashed the giant, flaming words repeatedly across the sky:

"WELCOME, PRINCE OF PEACE! WELCOME, THE FIRST BEGOTTEN OF THE DEAD! WELCOME, LION OF THE TRIBE OF JUDAH!"

Then came the sound of the voice of a multitude singing, like a choir, but the voices were of heavenly hosts, of multitude of angels all spotlessly white, thousands upon thousands upon thousands of them with brilliantly shining wings, surrounding the Saviour, and singing:

"GLORY TO GOD IN THE HIGHEST! AND TO HIS SON, THE LAMB, THE PRINCE OF PEACE, WHO THROUGH HIS OWN BLOOD, RANSOMED ALL HUMANITY BACK TO GOD!"

Lucifer, the fallen Angel, beheld all the spectacles and the wondrous glories in the heavens around the Saviour, and panicked severely. He knew this time, he had carried his wiles one time too far; he knew he had bitten off far more than he could possibly chew, for he knew this was something much bigger, much hotter than he could ever handle, for it seemed as though heavenly hosts were gathering against him and his little group of demons.

"Welcome, King of Kings!" A voice, sweet and unseen, suddenly said aloud, "Welcome, o root of Jesse! Thou indeed hath said that thou shall come again like a thief in the night…hast thou indeed return, o son of the living God, to judge the living and the dead on the earth?"

After a while, the wonderfully sweet and kingly voice of the Saviour, responded:

"Nay, thou inquisitive Sprite. The Son of Man cometh now just to attend to one specific purpose only, and shall return to the Father thereafter. The hour of judgment is yet delayed that all men and women, as many as cometh to Me, will I in no wise cast out."

Then in a sudden, the Lord of the Universes raised His right hand, and instantly, all the noises, all the praises by the elements, and all the singing by the angels, ceased altogether. Then the millions of white shining angels around Him all vanished in an instant. There was absolute silence now, a hallowed silence. The Lord was quite alone now, for He desired it that way.

II

Obinna Kelechi lay dead in his room. To any observer, who might have per chanced seen what was about to happen here, the room where Obinna died seemed to open up mysteriously, and the roof was no longer visible, and beyond was the night sky, completely lit up by the glory of the Son of God like the sun shining in full strength.

The Dark Angel and his cohorts, still stunned by what they had witnessed in the sky, were suddenly drawn fiercely away from Obinna's deathbed, where his Soul floated, by a very powerful mysterious and irresistible force at a commanding gesture from the Son of God, and were cast down instantly beneath His divine feet.

THE PACT

Then the Dark Angel, completely stunned and awestruck, stood up and looked up, but was too dismayed, too stunned, to speak. It was indeed a very frightening scene for any mortal observer to behold. But to God be the glory as everyone living in this part of the world had been put to an unusually-deep slumber.

The Prince of Peace stood on one side and the Prince of Darkness on the other. It was a glorious re-enactment of almost the same event that took place on the Mount of Temptation, millennia ago, when the Saviour of the world, then garbed in mortal flesh, stood face-to-face with the tempter of the world who tempted Him repeatedly with bread and with the gift of the glory of the world. How absurd! To be tempted with bread when He fed thousands with bread; to be tempted with the glory of the world when the world, with all its glory, were His, nay, a thousand billion worlds with their eternal glories were all His and His alone as He is heir alone of the Everlasting Father!

And what was in contention here? What was the reason for this colossal face-off to which hardly anything else on the earth could be compared in modern times? The Soul of one Obinna Kelechi who had just died!

What could be more worthless? Had Obinna Kelechi himself, when still alive, long before he became a believer in Jesus Christ, while he yet lived in his blind ignorance and senseless pride, not pronounced his own Soul as worthless? That Unbeliever! Atheist! Doubter! And Scoffer who dared to question and arrogantly deny the very existence of the Saviour Himself and of His Father for the most part of his miserable little life!

Perhaps to us humans, that Soul (Obinna's Soul) was worthless, but to the Creator of Souls, all Souls are worthy—of exceeding value—for did He not say that not even a single sparrow can fall to the ground without His Father's notice? And that we are of far more value than many sparrows! Thank God for His ever-forgiving heart. And like a prominent world figure said a few years ago, "Christ has a soft spot for the human race!" Thank God again for His soft spot for the human race.

All of a sudden, a mysterious something—something unnameable, something indescribable—suddenly appeared in the eyes of the Prince of Peace! And what was that in the eyes of the Son of God? For His eyes suddenly shone like a thousand million suns shinning in full strength! Then suddenly again, the glory around Him took on a million hues which radiated forth like a thousand million rainbows that coloured up the entire night sky very intensely in the dazzling colours of the brilliant rainbow!

The Dark Angel looked, saw it all, and even himself, proud and rebellious as he was, marvelled greatly, in spite of himself, at the wondrous glory that surrounded the Saviour of the world. Then he fell once again, with all his host of fallen Angels with him, beneath the feet of the Son of God.

He stood up once more, and this time, he attempted to speak. As he opened his mouth to speak, another commanding gesture from the Son of God stopped his mouth, and he was instantly struck with dumbness.

Then the Saviour spoke, His voice—infinitely sweet, infinitely tender—and vibrated very sweetly as though through the whole of eternity, saying:

"Lucifer, Son of the Morning, only once art thou permitted to speak."

These words of the Lord were followed by a mysterious silence, a silence with a depth inexpressible in words.

"Lucifer," the Saviour spoke again, *"Now at this hour art thou permitted to speak... Speak!"*

The Dark Angel's tongue loosened instantly, and he regained his voice. He opened his mouth and said:

"Thou Christ, Son of the Everlasting Father, I pray thee not to judge poor Lucifer too harshly. Why art thou out here? Is it on account of the jester known as Obinna Kelechi? That blind and arrogant fool! ...so brazenly ignorant, in spite of all his vaunted learning and everything he claimed to know; he was pitifully ignorant of the existence of the spiritual realm and all that happens there! I came hither that I might claim his Soul which in his gross stupidity he sold to me for riches which I freely bestowed upon him while he yet liveth on the earth in his profound vanity. He sold his Soul to me in a Pact that was binding for eternity."

Another silence followed.

"Thou Christ," he resumed again, "Greatly beloved of God, ought not be out here in the open on account of the damned Soul of Obinna Kelechi for it is not worth thy trouble. That Soul belongeth to Lucifer! All spirits bore witness to the signing and sealing of the Pact!"

Then the Saviour responded, His voice as sweet as ever with such sweetness that could have resurrected a thousand million long dead corpses.

"Lucifer," He said, *"When wilt thou cease from thy wiles, thou damned tempter? Thou*

deceiveth the children of My Father, all of whom I love dearly, with thy wretched wealth, and steal their Souls from them. What thou knowest not was that the man, Obinna Kelechi, did later reject thee completely; repented of his follies, and invited Me into his life while he yet liveth. He repented and turned in earnest to the Son of God. The moment he accepted Me into his life, Lucifer, I, the Lamb of God, whose blood was shed for him and his likes, did break thy pact with him to pieces and cast it completely asunder into absolute nothingness. Surely, Lucifer, I allowed thee to take his life; but the Soul which liveth forever, that will I take! The Son of Man shall not suffer the Soul of Obinna Kelechi into perdition because he repented of his sins and rejected thee! No, Lucifer! I forbid thee to touch, or even go near the Soul of Obinna Kelechi, that Soul is Mine!"

The Dark Angel heard these words, and was highly dismayed.

"Thou Christ," he started again, "Son of the Everlasting God, why doth thou care about worthless Souls? That Soul is damned and is no good to thee. It is a tainted one! Eternal Spirits bore witness to my Pact with that Soul; now will thou take it away from poor Lucifer just because thou canst?"

"Verily I say unto thee, Lucifer, no Soul is worthless before My Father and before Me; and on account of all Souls was My blood shed!"

Then the Lord raised His two arms in the air, arms supremely majestic, and showed His hands to the tempter.

"See, Lucifer," The golden voice said, *"See My hands where the nails bore through them. I was crucified for Obinna Kelechi's sake and for the sakes of all those who believe and will believe in Me."*

Thereafter, he raised the golden crown upon which were visibly inscribed the words, "King of Kings and Lord of Lords," from His head, thus exposing the splendidly beautiful head. The scar of the thorny crown, worn over His head by his executors, as they ridiculed him, just before His crucifixion, was there.

"See, Lucifer," the kingly voice said again, *"See My brow! See the mark left by the Crown of Thorns upon My brow!"*

Then He replaced the golden crown on His divine head in one graceful movement.

The Dark Angel merely watched Him in mixed admiration and stupefaction.

"Everything I suffered," The Lord said, *"Was for Obinna Kelechi and for all of mankind. In regard to thy pact with him; which thou sayest, so boastfully and so assuredly, was witnessed by the immortal spirits. Verily, I say unto thee, Satan, that the Son of God is the Creator and Lord over all Souls, even all spirits! Every immortal spirit bow and worship Me, even those spirits, Lucifer, which thou called to witness thy wicked pact, all bow to Me. Thy pact, o Lucifer, have I completely destroyed!"*

There was a long pause as Lucifer, completely overwhelmed by the glory of the Lord, felt absolutely powerless, helpless, and had nothing else he could possibly complain or protest about again. He merely stood watching the Saviour in utter amazement.

Then suddenly, the Lord's golden voice—infinitely sweet yet infinitely commanding—rang out the regal command:

"Get thee hence, Satan! Thou and all the fallen Angels with thee—away with thee into the abyss—and await the judgement that My Father hath prepared for thee."

Immediately, and with a loud cry, the Dark Angel with his host of demons fled from the presence of the Son of God.

III

Thereafter, the divine eyes of the Son of God—eyes so wonderfully beautiful, so wonderfully tender, and so full of forgiveness—were riveted in the direction where the Soul of Obinna Kelechi floated. The Soul was fully conscious and alive! But it was shy and overwhelmed with guilt; riddled with insecurities, unsure of its fate at the hands of the Lord of the Universes.

It was so conscious of its own shortcomings, its own sins, in the fifty years it lived on the earth when it animated Obinna Kelechi's body, that it could not even return the Lord's look of love and compassion, unsure of what His verdict might be. Many indeed were its sins, its blasphemies, but the one that grieved it so much more than all the others was the Pact which it signed and sealed with the Prince of Darkness, because it entered into that Pact out of the bold and senseless denial of the existence of the Son of God who now stood before it as Judge and crowned Lord of all created things in the Universe, all things seen and unseen. The Soul suddenly trembled severely with profound dread at the presence of the Prince of Peace.

While Obinna's Soul trembled; a smile suddenly lit up the heavenly-beautiful face of the Creator of Souls—a smile so sweet, so warm, so tender and so sympathetic—that the entire earth would have melted at the love, kindness and forgiveness expressed so wonderfully in it. Suddenly, He beckoned on the shy Soul, and with the smile still radiating powerfully from His Face; He said:

"Come hither! Come with Me, My child, to My Father's House, for in My Father's House, there are many mansions!"

The Soul's fears, its uncertainties, vanished instantly and were replaced by a rapturous calm as the words of Christ floated to it... words that drifted sweetly from lips divine, and which seemed to echo to the very ends of the earth. And while the Soul revelled in this blissful peace, realizing that all its sins were forgiven, the sound of *Gloria in Excelsis,* sang by uncountable and unseen celestial voices, suddenly broke out upon the hallowed silence. The very air itself seemed to reverberate with the hymn. It is indeed a fact that there is much rejoicing in heaven over a single soul that repents of its sins.

As the Soul marvelled greatly at the beautiful singing of heavenly hosts, once again, the divine voice of the Son of God said:

"Come hither!"

In response; the Soul drifted upwards, floating freely and unhindered, into the clouds to meet the Redeemer. The moment it reached where He stood, it fell at His feet and worshipped Him.

"Well done!" The Saviour said to the Soul. *"Well done, thou faithful servant. Because thou believeth in Me, even unto death, I shall give thee the Keys of the Kingdom. Arise to thy feet, come now with Me, and enter into the everlasting joys of thy Lord."*

"Thank you, Lord." The Soul muttered as it rose slowly to its feet in obedience, "Thank you, O Lamb of God, for taking away my sins and the sins of the world."

Then they moved together in the clouds: The Prince of Peace—majestic, supreme and grand—clothed with unspeakable splendour led the way; whilst Obinna Kelechi's Soul drifted behind Him till they entered the furthermost clouds and were seen no more.

The End

EPILOGUE

Obinna Kelechi's body was discovered later in the room where he had hidden himself. His servants forced the door open and there he was, very dead, at the prime age of fifty years; but looking peaceful with a faint smile on his face. His dear wife, Monica, was completely broken-hearted and so was his friend, the beloved Martha.

None knew, none suspected, or had the slightest inkling of the terrifying encounter, or of its incredible magnitude, that had taken place, in the dead of night, over the Soul of the man whose smiling body lay dead on the bed—victorious in death—through the forgiveness and love of Jesus Christ: the divine friend, brother, helper and redeemer of mankind.

Two weeks later, Obinna Kelechi was buried according to Christian rites.

At the funeral ceremony, when all the guests had departed, two people still lingered on at his graveside—his wife, Monica and his friend, Martha—the two women in his life who had influenced him the most. Their eyes were moist with tears; and the heaviness in their hearts, very profound indeed. After a while, the two women, without uttering any word, started walking very slowly away from the graveside, leaning tenderly on each other's arm.

www.ingramcontent.com/pod-product-compliance
Lightning Source LLC
LaVergne TN
LVHW021652060526
838200LV00050B/2325